Got It
Going On

Also by Stephanie Perry Moore

Perry Skky Jr. series

Prime Choice
Pressing Hard
Problem Solved
Prayed Up
Promise Kept

Beta Gamma Pi series

Work What You Got
The Way We Roll
Act Like You Know

Got It Going On

A Beta Gamma Pi Novel
Book 4

Stephanie Perry Moore

KENSINGTON PUBLISHING CORP.

www.kensingtonbooks.com

DAFINA BOOKS are published by

Kensington Publishing Corp.
119 West 40th Street
New York, NY 10018

All Kensington titles, imprints, and distributed lines are available at special quantity discounts for bulk purchases for sales promotion, premiums, fund-raising, educational, or institutional use.

Special book excerpts or customized printings can also be created to fit specific needs. For details, write or phone the office of the Kensington Special Sales Manager: Kensington Publishing Corp., 119 West 40th Street, New York, NY 10018. Attn. Special Sales Department. Phone: 1-800-221-2647.

Kensington and the K logo Reg. U.S. Pat. & TM Off.

ISBN-13: 978-0-7582-3445-2
ISBN-10: 0-7582-3445-7

First Kensington Trade Paperback Printing: January 2010
10 9 8 7 6 5 4 3 2 1

Printed in the United States of America

In loving memory of
Cleo Armstrong (a Delta whose will I was in),
Beatrice Blue (a Delta whose paro I have),
Louise Lindsey (my godmother's mom),
Lizzie Mae Perry (my paternal grandma),
and Viola Roundtree (my maternal grandma)—
the five women who are the basis for
the founders of this series

You gems made this world richer with your
grace, love, and wisdom!
Standing on your shoulders has helped me learn
what it truly means to have it going on.
You all lived long, wonderful lives filled with so much.
But the collective lesson you taught me is,
above all, to love God most.
May all readers strive for their dreams but
get that crucial point etched in their hearts.

ACKNOWLEDGMENTS

Predominantly African American Greek organizations were founded on Christian principles. What a wonderful thing! With God in the middle of the groups, they can't go off track. Unfortunately, the devil is real, and he comes to kill, steal, and destroy. So unless the groups stay grounded and remember their purpose, they fall into sin: hazing, hatred, and devilish ways. Unless God is a part of the sorority or fraternity, the members will fail miserably and add up to much less than their founders intended. This book was written to show why God is needed every step of the way.

Writing a novel about what happens when college students sin was tough. Honestly, I wasn't a Goody Two-shoes in college and was far from perfect. However, that's the joy in knowing Christ. With Him, you can fall—but you can get back up and have an even stronger walk in the end. To truly have it going on doesn't mean you're popular, rich, or smart. It means you know He is the only One who can save your soul. The meaning, purpose, and identity you long for is in Him. Don't get me wrong, being Greek can get you a long way. But being a part of God's family will take you all the way and is all that matters. Here is a big shout-out to those who pray for me and walk with me throughout every step of my writing journey.

For my family: parents Dr. Franklin and Shirley Perry, Sr.; brother Dennis and sister-in-law Leslie; nephew Franklin III; mother-in-law Ms. Ann; and extended family Reverend and Mrs. Kimbrough, Bobby and Sarah Lundy, Antonio and Gloria London, Cedric and Nicole Smith, Harry and Nino Colon, Brett and Loni Perriman, Chandra Dixon, Lakeba Williams, and Michele Clark Jenkins—thank you for praying for my strength. May every college student feel as secure as your support makes me.

For my publisher, Kensington/Dafina Books, and especially Laurie Parkin, thank you for answering my prayer and having me at this great house. May every person know he or she can be successful after they leave school.

For my writing team: Ciara Roundtree, Ashley Duncan, Chantel Morgan, and Alyx Pinkston—thank you for praying for my work and coming through to make it better. May all readers learn to surround themselves with hardworking people who believe in their dreams.

For my DST sorors, for whom I care deeply, especially my special sisters: Victoria Christopher Murray, Trevy McDonald, Jenell Clark, Deborah Thomas, Christine Nixon, Myra Brown, Anita Gasden, Kara Wright, Celeste Jordan, Debra Abernathy, Cassandra Brown, Isha Western, Pam Murphy, Dayna Fleming, Yolanda Rogers-Hauser, Anita Shaw, Marcia Butler-Holt, Cynthia Boyd, and in memory of Brenda Haywood—thank you for praying for me to keep going. May all collegiate Greeks, especially our Deltas, know they can make it and enjoy the climb.

For my children: Dustyn Leon, Sydni Derek, and Sheldyn Ashli—thank you for praying for Mommy's dreams to come true. May every young person know that what he or she does today affects generations to come.

For my hubby, Derrick Moore, thank you for praying for my breakthrough. May every person have a cheerleader like you in his or her corner.

For my readers, thank you for trying this series, as that alone is an answer to my prayers as well. May each of you know the world is waiting on you to do your thing and make this place better.

And for Jesus, thank You for praying for my soul and for dying for my sins. May every person know You are all that matters.

BETA GAMMA PI
TRADITIONS, CUSTOMS, & RITES

Founding Data

Beta Gamma Pi was founded in 1919 on the campus of Western Smith College by five extraordinary women of character and virtue.

Sorority Colors

Sunrise lavender and sunset turquoise are the official colors of Beta Gamma Pi. The colors symbolize the beginning and the end of the swiftly passing day and remind each member to make the most of every moment.

Sorority Pin

Designed in 1919, the pin is made of the Greek letters Beta, Gamma, and Pi. This sterling silver pin is to be worn over the heart on the outermost garment. There are five stones in the Gamma: a ruby representing courageous leadership, a pink tourmaline representing genuine sisterhood, an emerald representing a profound education, a purple amethyst representing deep spirituality, and a blue sapphire representing unending service.

Anytime the pin is worn, members should conduct themselves with dignity and honor.

The B Pin

The B Pin was designed in 1920 by the founders. This basic silver pin in the shape of the letter B symbolizes the beginning step in the membership process. The straight side signifies character. The two curves mean yielding to God and yielding to others. It is given at the Pi Induction Ceremony.

Sorority Flower

The lily is the sorority flower and it denotes the endurance and strength the member will need to be a part of Beta Gamma Pi for a lifetime.

Sorority Stone

The diamond is the sorority stone, which embodies the precious and pure heart needed to be a productive member of Beta Gamma Pi.

Sorority Call

Bee-goh-p

Sorority Symbol

The eagle is the symbol of Beta Gamma Pi. It reflects the soaring greatness each member is destined to reach.

Sorority Motto

A sisterhood committed to making the world greater.

The Pi Symbol

The Bee insect is the symbol of the Pi pledges. This symbolizes the soaring tenacity one must possess to become a full member of Beta Gamma Pi.

Contents

BENEVOLENT

*Y*eah, I know I got it going on, and even with all the eyes rolling my way, I'm not gonna feel bad about that. My dark, almond-toned skin is glazed to perfection. My 5'7" body is slim in all the right places. My sassy short do moves the men. I know how to work it. Every guy at this Student Government Association back-to-school party is checking me out, including the fine, commanding SGA president, Al Dutch.

Al Dutch—yes, he wants everyone to use his whole name all the time, saying he plans to run for political office one day and we need to remember him. Al is a lady's man; he looks, walks, and talks like money! You know the type. The one who's confident and cocky and always has a sure smile plastered on his or her face, with a no-worry, got-much-loot look in his or her eyes. Al's that type. His skin glows like he has slept on the best satin sheets and used the finest body oils all his life. All the men wanna be him. All the girls wanna be with him—including me. It was game time, and I was flirting hard.

Western Smith is your typical historically black college with even more bells and whistles. We are rich in history in our great state of Arkansas. We have everything at our disposal—a good football team, excellent academics, amazing Greek life, and great cultural campus events. Western Smith even has a first-rate band—which is the place where I fit most.

I was a drum major my sophomore year. Now that I'm a junior, I've switched gears and decided to try something different. Now I'm captain of the dance team. One would think my life is perfect, but my reputation isn't the best. Though I don't care what people think or say about me, I know I want to make the line of Beta Gamma Pi. Three years ago when I first came to college, I was at a probate show where the sisters were stepping, and I remember all the excited oohs and ahhs they received from the crowd. It was then that I knew I really wanted to be a Beta. Plus, their sorors in my hometown of Natchez, Mississippi, helped get me through my high school years and because of their scholarship, I was able to attend Western Smith.

After meeting some Betas in middle school, I had researched the sorority. I found newspaper clippings about the five founders, and I'd even taken a tour of the National Headquarters about thirty miles from campus. The more I looked into what the Betas were all about—leadership, sisterhood, education, Christianity, and public service—I knew they were the sorority for me. The whole God thing wasn't really my thing, but I knew to be a Beta, I had to either clean up my act and hope they would vote me in or cancel that dream altogether.

"Oooo, girl, you working it. Making a brothah lose his mind. Let's get outta here," Al Dutch said as he grabbed my waist after I sashayed my body all around his in a seductive manner.

"Boy, please. I don't even know you like that," I said.

With the stare of a tiger hungry to eat, Al Dutch said, "Oh, you know exactly who I am. And I know you, Ms. Cassidy Cross. And you want everything I got to give. Don't play. I chose you tonight, baby. Now, you see all the ladies' eyes are focused on me, and if I made the wrong choice you need to let me know now, and I'll be on my way."

I looked around me, and he was right. There were girls just waiting for the chance to talk to Al Dutch. But even though I wasn't ready to groove with him between the sheets, I could move my body on the dance floor.

"Come here. You can't make up your mind?" he said. Then he pointed in the direction of a girl who was on the dance team with me, Miss Ginger. I didn't know her well, but I knew she didn't like the fact that I was chosen to head up the dance team. She'd thought she would have the honor because of seniority—she had been on the team the last two years. However, I'd had the moves in my favor, and I'd ultimately won out. I could see the anger in her face from across the room. She was cute, but Al Dutch was jocking me and obviously thought I was cuter.

"Come on, let's go," I said, tugging him back to me and wrapping his arm around my waist to piss her off more.

"That's what I'm talking about," he said to me as he laid a sloppy kiss on my lips in front of the crowd.

I was taken aback by his bold move, but with so many girls after him, I guess he was used to getting what he wanted. I hadn't seen any Betas in the house to use this against me. They didn't like to see prospective members being too sassy in public. So before they came to this jumping party, Al Dutch and I left.

I'd come to the party with my roommate, and she knew the drill—if I didn't meet up with her once the party was over, she knew I'd catch up with her at home. So I didn't sweat looking for her—though, once I got in his car and he lit a joint and handed it to me, I wondered if I should have told my girl where I was. I wanted to have a good time, but I wasn't into smoking pot.

Although it was a ten-minute ride to his crib, he barely said two words to me. Al Dutch was what most girls at Western Smith dreamed of, but right now, smoking a joint, he wasn't being dreamy, just careless.

When we arrived at his apartment, it was confirmed that the boy was loaded. His crib was huge. The living room area was decked out with a fifty-inch plasma TV. His kitchen had all the finest appliances, from the stainless-steel microwave to the automatic dishwasher. The wall-to-wall carpet was thick and plush and clean. I strolled down the hallway and entered the master bedroom. The green-and-brown color scheme went along with his tasteful style. I was in awe as I enjoyed the view and made my way back to the fine brother I was ready to spend the rest of the evening talking to.

"Don't get me wrong, this is my parents' place, but I'm a business major, and when I learn enough to take over the family business I will own *all* this," he said. "My parents own Dutch Cosmetics, one of the most successful African American beauty lines. But as pretty as your beautiful skin is, I don't think we have anything that could make you more gorgeous."

Dutch then came over to the couch, put his arms around me, and went in for a kiss. Again, we hadn't said much to each other. I needed him to back the heck off, but he was so aggressive. His hands were all over me, and before I knew it, my shirt was off, and he was trying to take off my pants. This wasn't what I wanted, so I shoved him away from me.

With my hands in front of me, I said, "Stop! I'm not ready for this yet; I want to get to know you. Please stop."

"Girl, please. I hope you didn't think I brought you over here so we could talk," he said as I tried to cover myself. "Oh, no, ain't no need to hide all that. Tonight you're mine. Look around—you best believe I get what I want."

With that, he picked me up and took me to his bedroom, where he threw me down on his king-size bed. He wouldn't take no for an answer, no matter how much I tried to stop him. So I just laid there feeling practically dead inside.

* * *

"Ugh, what are you looking at?" Al Dutch questioned me twenty minutes later.

Instantly, I hung my head low. He was a jerk, and I was both angry and saddened. *Did I ask for this?* I wondered, unable to move.

"We're done," he said in a disgusted voice.

I felt like my insides were ripped apart. He had a satisfied grin on his face, but I felt devastated. Though I was angry, I didn't act on it. I just lay there.

"Cassidy, can you not hear? You ain't getting round two. Put your clothes on," he said as he threw them in my face. "I got someone else coming through in a few, so I need you to get up outta my space."

I still couldn't move. He walked over toward me and tried to grab me. I jerked away from him. I didn't want him touching me again, not after what he'd just done to me. The instant he tried to touch me, it was like I unthawed and was on fire. I quickly got up, grabbed my stuff, and headed to the nearest door, not caring where it led to.

Entering the bathroom, I looked in the mirror and said softly, "How did you let this happen, Cass?"

All I wanted was a man to love me. I deeply wanted a family someday. I knew the altercation with Al Dutch was a real indication that I wasn't doing things the proper way. The hours leading up to this quickly zoomed through my memory. The girl he'd left with at the party had seemed up for anything. I had totally sent out the wrong signals.

I so wanted to be a Beta. I was thinking back to the

conversation I had had last school year with Alyx Cruz, the new transfer Beta who had it going on and was rumored to be the head of the line. She had told me I shouldn't give people a reason to think I was fast. And with Al Dutch I'd only done what I'd always done—been carefree and not taken things so seriously. But as I looked in the mirror, I realized no sorority was gonna want me if I had let a guy like Al Dutch do what he'd done to me. Replaying the scene over and over, I hated myself.

"For real, you gotta go. You need to leave!" Al Dutch said, interrupting my thoughts. "Your teammate, Meagan, is headed over here. I gotta do her. This ain't nothing like love, and it wasn't even that good, so get out!"

Wow, what was he planning on doing? Getting with all the girls on the dance team? Ginger had been eyeing him down at the party. Now he was talking about getting with Meagan. This guy was nasty.

Dang! I threw water on my face and stared at myself one last time in his bathroom mirror. I knew this was the moment I needed to change. I opened the door, fully dressed, and walked out.

"Are you crying? What, you thought I wanted a relationship? You mean nothing to me. I gave you the night you wanted."

Finally, I went for the attack—took my hand and grabbed his neck. "You raped me."

"What? You're dreaming," he said. "You asked for it in every way." He took my arm and twisted it behind my back. "And don't you even think about going to the cops."

"Stop!" I shouted in agony. "You're hurting me! Let go!"

"Not until you understand that you don't need to be making no remarks like that. Everybody at the party saw you coming on to me and eyeing me down. Don't try to cry rape now. I gave you everything you asked for. You're sorry now, and you just need to deal with it. Now for the last time, get out and leave me out of it."

I didn't know if I could do that, but I knew I had to leave. I jetted to the front door, hating all that had happened.

When I reached my apartment, I felt worthless. My hands were trembling so badly I could barely open the front door, and eventually my roommate, Samantha Kelly, came to help. She was a cool girl from Alabama who had grandparents in Arkansas. She was really laid back and relaxed, so she was always able to calm me down.

"Cass, what are you doing? Girl, I didn't know who was out here messing with the doorknob," she said while holding on to the steel bat we kept at the door for protection.

She played softball at our school and, like me, she wanted to pledge Beta Gamma Pi. Without noticing something was wrong with me, she blabbed about an upcoming Beta event.

"I was hoping you'd get here soon. A lot of us who are trying to pledge Beta are getting together to discuss if they've heard word of the Betas having a line. A fall line, that is. Because they didn't have a line last year, this is supposed to be the biggest line to be brought over. Are you listening to me?" she asked when I stared at the bare wall instead of at her face. She finally realized I was in a daze. She reached out to hug me, and I jerked back. "What's wrong? Talk to me, Cass."

I wanted so badly to blurt out, *"I've been raped! Just help me!"* but my body helplessly fell to the floor.

She was reluctant to hug me again. "Please talk to me, Cassidy, please." Her phone rang. "It's some of the girls. They wanna talk about the Beta Gamma Pi thing, but I don't wanna leave you alone. Something's not right. Was it Al Dutch? I saw you with him at the party, and you guys were hot and heavy. Then I saw you leave with him. Did he hurt you?"

In a whisper, I uttered, "I wish he'd left me alone and looked in another direction, talked to another girl or something."

"Did things not go well? Did he reject you?" she asked, now seriously concerned.

I looked over at her, held my stomach, and said, "I wish he'd done anything but what he did."

"You guys looked really into each other. So many of the girls from Beta Gamma Pi came up to me and asked if you knew what you were doing because you're not supposed to come off as promiscuous."

I looked up with tears in my eyes and said, "So because I was a little flirty, that meant I wanted to give it up to him, that it was okay for him take it? My consent out on the dance floor gave him a reason to rape me?"

"What?" she said, reaching for me again.

"I—" I couldn't even finish, and I just started bawling. She held me in her arms. "Cass, I'm so sorry, baby. I didn't know. We gotta call the police. You have to report this. You gotta get to the hospital. Even though he's our SGA president, you can't let him get away with this."

"Ugh! Just leave. I don't want you to get involved, and I don't wanna talk about this anymore. Just go."

"I'm not gonna leave you like this. We're going to the hospital," Sam insisted as she tugged me toward the door.

Removing her hand from my shirt, I shouted, "I'm not going anywhere! You said it yourself that no one's gonna believe me, and I practically asked for it. Go!"

I guess I yelled and screamed enough because she finally left me by myself. Before I could even get to the bathroom and soak in the shower to get his stench off me, I went into the kitchen and just collapsed in a heaping, crying ball.

GARBAGE

Sam must have heard my cries because she came running back into the kitchen. "Oh, my gosh! Cassie, what's going on, girl? Something told me to come back here. I shouldn't have left you alone."

I was just trembling, unable to comprehend what was happening. I was so weak I couldn't hold myself up. Emotionally exhausted, I cried, "I don't wanna be here. I don't wanna feel like this. I just let a man rape me. What's wrong with me?"

All of a sudden I heard Sam praying behind me. "Lord, you gotta help my roommate. She experienced something awful tonight and doesn't know how to cope. Help her to see it through, Lord. Please, help her know You're here. Help her know You care. I love her so much, and I can't lose her. If You're listening, Lord, and I know You're listening, help her."

I have never been someone to sit and talk with the Lord and let Him know how I feel. Maybe if I did, I wouldn't have felt so empty right now. I admired that Sam believed He was real. Though I wasn't ready to make that leap of faith and commit, I was intrigued that she had gone to her God on my behalf. It did something to me that I couldn't explain. It was like I found Cassidy Cross again. Though I was so shaken, so vulnerable, and so scared, I was stable.

"Thank you," I said, wiping the tears from my eyes.

"Are you sure you're okay?" Sam questioned.

"Yes," I insisted, realizing now that after receiving her help, I did feel better.

Sam began to make some soup for me. As she cooked, we chatted over warm tea, but throughout our conversation, Sam's cell phone kept ringing.

"Somebody's trying to get you. Don't you think you need to answer?" I asked her.

"It's all right. I'd rather be here for you right now."

"Thank you. But I feel different now. It's time for me to take responsibility for my actions. It's obvious that you can't judge a book by its cover. I was being so naive, and I thought Al Dutch was this great guy. I don't know. I do know that this was an eye-opening experience for me, though."

As we sat in the living room, we continued talking. Sam didn't want me out of her sight, so we talked until we could talk no more and fell asleep on the couch.

Sam's phone rang, awakening us at three in the afternoon the next day, and she was irritated when she checked the number. "Ugh! They're just going to have to go on without me."

"What—who's going to have to go on without you?" I asked.

"The Betas are having their Party Till Dawn back-to-school jam tonight, and they expect all of us prospects to be there if we want to be on the line. How can I go now? You being okay is more important to me than going to some party," Sam said, though I could tell she was disappointed about not being able to go to the Beta party.

"Wow. Girl, you are a better roommate to me than I am to you," I said to her, digging her loyalty.

"What are you talking about, Cass?"

"I don't know. You're saying you're not going to the Beta party, which is something you passionately wanna be a part of. Instead you would rather make sure I'm all right. I mean, we've always been cool, but we hang in different circles. I didn't know you had my back like that."

"Well, I would love for you to hang out with my friends. People do look down on us because we don't wear the coolest clothes and we look like nerds, but we don't mind. Though being a member of Beta Gamma Pi is what I really want, I could never live with myself if I wasn't there for you tonight." She came over and held my hands. "Don't believe what anybody has to say about you. You are worth something."

"Thanks. I guess I just felt like his trash."

"I'm kinda upset that you're not gonna press charges, but then I do understand the concept of it all. Are you sure you're okay, Cassidy?" Sam asked sincerely.

"Yes, I gotta just think better, do better, be better. I know that my actions have consequences. I'm happy that I got a roommate who really cares, but I'm not going to let you stay here and miss the party because of me. Have fun, girl."

Putting her hand on her hip, Sam said defiantly, "Oh, no. I'm not leaving you again."

"Well, I guess I'm going then." I got up. "I'm not going to hold you back. We're in this pledging thing together. I'm not all right, but sitting here sulking is not gonna help me be all right either."

So I felt like I'd been run over repeatedly by a Mack truck, yet there I stood at the Beta Gamma Pi bash. My self-esteem was low to the ground, and my dignity had been thrown out of the window. Being at this Beta party reminded me of the events that had taken place the previous night. I didn't want to be there, but I was pulling for Sam, and I also didn't want to completely ruin my own chances of pledging Beta.

"Oh, my gosh! There are more people here than at the SGA party last night. Oooo, we're gonna have a good time!" Sam said to me.

I didn't even respond. She was way too excited. I kept my mouth shut, and I let her continue to admire the scene. I had just been through something awful, and as I looked at the Betas checking every one of us out, I thought, *This ain't even worth it. They think I'm crap, and I feel like trash, so what's the point of even trying to be a part of their sorority?*

As soon as I turned around, Alyx Cruz, the cool Spanish Beta girl who had given me advice, smiled at me. She lifted her chin as if to say everything was gonna be all right.

I just wished I could go back in time and replay my actions. I hadn't had anything to drink, so I hadn't been tipsy. I knew what I was doing. I wanted Al Dutch to notice me and make me his girl. But when he'd taken it a step further and taken advantage of me like I was nothing, it was dead wrong, and he needed to pay the consequences.

"Now, you look like you're ready to jump on somebody. See, I told you you shouldn't have come. You should've rested and stayed home," Sam said loudly.

I gave Sam a sharp look. She didn't need to tell my business to everyone within hearing distance. It wasn't only that—I appreciated her concern—but this was my mess, and I needed to work through this alone. I didn't need anyone holding my hand through this outrageous ordeal. This was my own battle I had to fight.

There was absolutely no way I was going to be able to erase life's events from my mind. I was going through a roller coaster of emotions, and I knew if I saw Al Dutch at that moment it wouldn't be myself I was trying to take out of this world. It would be Al Dutch.

"Um, did you know the dance team was coming tonight?" Sam said, trying to quickly change the subject, pointing to the door.

I was speechless. Here I was, captain of the dance team, and there were all nine of them dressed alike, with tight shirts and miniskirts, doing a little strut. Finally, I answered her question. "No, I didn't. I'm gonna go over and see what's up. I'll be back."

"Yeah, I'm gonna get up with my crew and see if the Betas need us to get more refreshments, help out the deejay, or something. Don't want them to say I didn't offer to help."

I was confused for two reasons at this point. I mean, first, why did these Betas think they were above the law? They had only recently been allowed to hold pledging activities on campus again. We weren't supposed to be doing anything for them—even helping the deejay—until we were officially on line. Now, I could understand them making sure we supported their events—that was cool. But doing chores for them? That was hazing, and I wasn't doing it, and they shouldn't want me or Sam to, because if anybody found out about it, they would be in trouble. And word going around was if anything else negative got out about them, there would be no more Alpha chapter of Beta Gamma Pi. Everyone knew campus administration and Beta Gamma Pi's national officers had just granted them permission to be back on campus after being off the yard for serious hazing violations last year. Secondly, I couldn't believe my own dance team was here, and it was unbeknownst to me. I could see them looking at me. They had gall, and they looked stank with attitude. I needed some answers.

So I walked over to them, and the cocaptain, Ginger, got all in my face. I hadn't even said anything, and she was already giving me attitude. "What's the problem? Yeah, you're the captain, but we're not kids, and we don't need your permission for gigs. We're not in uniform, and we really don't wanna be led by someone with a reputation like yours, all on the dance floor with our SGA president like that. That was the last straw, and we want you out. Get away from us. We're discussing this with the band director on Monday."

The rest of the girls didn't say anything to collaborate with her story, but they didn't say anything to back me up either. Meagan wasn't there. I wondered if she was still with Al Dutch. Realizing it wasn't my concern either way and that I wasn't gonna let these jealous girls ruin my night, I walked away. I definitely didn't want to be anywhere I wasn't wanted. The bigger problem was I didn't know if I wanted to be around me either. Now I was down again. So far I was in a hole of doom, and I wasn't sure if there was a way out.

"I don't know why she's wearing a size eight when her butt knows she needs to be in a fourteen," I overheard Torian say to her line sister Loni. I looked around, and I realized they were talking about me.

We'd all been in school together for a few years, but Betas Torian and Loni were seniors. Though they hadn't had a line last year, I knew them well. The chapter President Malloy Murray, who was the National President's daughter, was standing right in the middle of them. I couldn't tell if she was laughing along with them, but she certainly wasn't defending me either. Torian continued.

"Look at her. Even her own dance members don't want her. She's the last one I'm voting into Beta Gamma Pi, for real. Did y'all hear how scandalous her dance moves were on the dance floor last night? And where has she been? Everybody and their mama know that Al Dutch is nasty!"

"You used to like him," Loni quickly reminded her friend.

Torian said, "Yeah, till I woke up and smelled the crap he was shooting out his tail. Ain't no telling what his tired behind got, and he wasn't gonna give it to me."

I rushed to the bathroom. I couldn't take it anymore. I hadn't even thought about the fact that this dude could've gotten me pregnant, given me an infection, or, even worse, given me AIDS. I just shook my head. It felt as if three pounds of oversize bricks had been dropped on me. So much of what had happened last night was messed up. And as the Betas pointed out, so much of it was my fault.

"What have I done?" I yelled out, thankful that no one else was in there.

I held my abdomen as the images of last night's events played over and over again in my mind. And now of course my mind was playing tricks on me because I threw up. Oh, no! Did this mean I was pregnant? *Settle down, Cassidy,* I told myself. *It's too early for you to be pregnant.* I went over to the sink and threw freezing water on my face. When I looked up, I realized water wasn't the only thing covering my face—it was now joined with warm tears. I felt worthless. So empty. Like nothing.

I put my head back down in the sink. I needed a hand to erase my anguish. I needed help figuring out where to go from here. Suddenly, as I rose, I was stunned to find Alyx Cruz behind me as if she'd heard my plea.

"You can't let them intimidate you," she said as she

placed her hand on my back. I had been so jittery lately that I didn't even know how to react. Her gesture was actually soothing, and I could tell Alyx was there for me as a friend.

"I messed up so badly," I cried to Alyx.

"We all make mistakes. None of us are perfect. And I know you came here tonight because Beta Gamma Pi is still in your heart. I'm only one person, not the chapter, so I can't promise anything. But I love your spirit and your vulnerability. You're real. A lot of these girls are jealous because they wish they could have some attention. Remember what I told you last year?" I shook my head, wanting her to repeat her words of wisdom. "Tone it down a little before you attract things you don't want."

She couldn't possibly know how powerful those words were for me right now. But it was too late. I had already dug myself into a hole I couldn't get out of.

"I can tell you want some time alone, so I'm not gonna stay." She took my hands. "But I just want you to understand that there will be times when we get to a place where we feel we have no hope. But I wanna tell you right now, whether you get to join Beta Gamma Pi or not, you are something special, so start living like it. Hold your head up high and remember that you're special and can be anything."

PURPOSE

It was two weeks later, and I was getting ready to head over to the Beta Gamma Pi rush event. I was hoping Sam was also going to attend. "So are we going to the Beta Gamma Pi rush together or not?" I asked Sam.

She just looked at me and rolled her eyes. It's funny what time can do. It took only a night for Al Dutch to turn me from wild, crazy, and daring to crude and boring Cassidy Cross. And it took two weeks for me and my roommate to get to the point where we couldn't stand being around each other.

"You don't have to be so mean about it," she said, being nicer than she'd been in the last couple days.

I didn't know why she was being sweet. After all, I wasn't crazy. I knew her girls had told her if she wanted to pledge she was going to have to cut me loose. Now that she knew I was gonna make it and deal with my tragedy on my own, she had to decide. Actions clearly spoke louder than words. For her to get herself where she wanted to be in life, I was a casualty she had to distance herself from.

"I'm just going to go with my friends, Cassidy. All right?" Sam said, not wanting to hurt my feelings.

I just shrugged my shoulders and walked away. I wasn't going to beg anybody to chill with them. She had chosen the other chicks, and that was fine with me. I could stand alone.

She followed me, touched my shoulder, and said, "You know, if this is for us, God will work it out. He cares about us, Cass. Trust that His plan for our lives is the one we need to follow."

I just looked at her. What was she talking about? See, that was my whole issue with Christian people. They were always thinking that God was going to work it out even when people didn't deserve grace.

I couldn't imagine, if there was some justified person ruling the world, that He'd be pleased with her actions. She wasn't rude to me, but she wasn't too friendly. Yeah, we could talk at home, but on campus she acted as if she didn't know me. We could be walking in the same direction toward class, but if she was with her friends, she would turn the other cheek and not acknowledge me at all. Where was the good in treating people like trash? When I had figured out what she was doing, I started giving her the ice-cold shoulder at home.

"You're straight. No need to explain or try to justify who you want to roll to the meeting with. I'll see you there. No worries," I said to her as she smiled, thinking everything was cool between us.

Whatever! Her girls had gotten into her ear, and I knew what the deal was. We shared the same space but not the same world. She just kept on primping. I grabbed my keys and jumped into my white Honda Accord and headed to the Betas' sorority room on campus for the rush.

I got there early. I was usually a punctual person, and this was no exception. The Betas who had mentored me back home had told me the importance of being timely. No CP Time, they'd always say. I guess it had stuck with me. So I sat in my car and chilled.

I watched the girls go by, both Betas and the ones who wanted to be in the group, and I pondered whether I still wanted to be a part of snooty Alpha chapter. Alpha chapter thought they were all that. And though they were cute, had style, and were academically on point, the air they gave off was so funky that smelling a sewer had nothing on it.

It was just so funny to me since they'd been through so much over the past few years. That Western Smith was the birthplace of the sorority was being overshadowed by the recent turmoil the girls had faced. Hazing charges, stalkers, and a tragic accident had taken a toll on the chapter, but even through all that, they had still bounced back, which was beyond me.

It had been so hard for me to sleep recently, and if I went to this rush and they didn't impress me, I was going to walk out, showing them where they could stick their letters. I was not interested in joining a group of women who cared more about primping than serving their community.

The doors were closing to their sorority room, and I'd just barely made it before Loni shut the door. She looked me up and down, and I could tell she was not happy I was almost late. I knew she thought she had what I wanted, but only I knew why I wanted to be a Beta so bad. It was the deep desire to serve with my whole heart. Loni may not have known it or believed it, but she needed me. I'd be an asset to Alpha chapter.

I was deeply impressed with the sorority room. It was the first time I'd ever been in there, so I was awestruck. I had walked by their closed front door several times all last year wondering what adorned the walls inside. Now I was in admiration looking at the gorgeous pictures of the founders. All five ladies in the black-and-white photo looked so lovely yet serious. Something in their eyes was enticing. I knew they were tired of things being the same in boring old Arkansas, and they had changed it. I'm sure they'd liked boys and loved grooving to cool sounds that were popular in their time, but on that picture before me it was clear their focus was on making the world better for their kind. Chills went up and down my back, and I thought about extending their dream.

My attention was deterred when someone from the front of the room called everyone to order. "Okay, if I can just have your attention. I'm Malloy Murray, chapter President. We're about to get started with the rush for the ladies of purple and turquoise. Could everyone take a seat, please?"

There were more than a hundred girls in the room. Clearly, this was going to be a big line. We were seated on one side of the room, and the Betas were in front of us, seated as well. I really didn't have anybody to hang out with so I sat alone with an empty seat between me and Sam's crew.

Malloy continued. "We're going to introduce ourselves to you, and then we'll have Torian come up and lead you all in an exercise so we can get to know you better. First, though, I'd like to introduce you to Dr. Garnes. She is our new chapter adviser and we're so honored to have her serve. She doesn't say much, but when she speaks it's powerful."

The lady waved at us, and we waved back before she stood and said, "Thanks, Malloy, for those kind words. Hello, ladies. As she said, I'm Dr. Garnes. I am here for you all as an adviser, and I do want you to know that no one should be involved in prehazing activities. If any Beta asks you to do anything, and I'm not around, it's not considered legitimate, and you should not comply. Any questions?"

Torian's eyes were rolling as she hit her buddy Loni in the arm. I could tell she wasn't feeling the adviser. I was happy though that the adviser was tough. Their old adviser had obviously been too soft on them, and thus they had been able to get into so much trouble.

Two rows in front of us was a girl sitting alone. She was jittery and twirling something in her hands. Sam's crew was laughing at her like they were all that. One girl in Sam's crew had on a dress that needed ironing. Another girl was in desperate need of a perm. And the other girl—the ringleader, named Cheryl—had horribly stained yellow teeth. I wasn't judging, but they didn't need to be laughing at nobody. They quickly hushed up when the Betas looked perturbed that they were being rude.

Because I already knew most of the Betas, when they were introducing themselves I fixed my attention back on the wall of pictures. The pictures on the purple partition illustrated how the sorority had grown over the years, and the real letters of signed past presidents throughout the room intrigued me. Of all the chapters of Beta Gamma Pi, being a member of Alpha chapter just added a little something special.

"All right, now we want to hear from you guys and find out why you want to be a part of Beta Gamma Pi," Torian said condescendingly, as if none of us could possibly give an answer that would merit impressing any of the Betas.

The girl next to Sam stood up and spoke first. "Hi, my name is Marietta, and I'm from Orangeburg, South Carolina. I love the parties you guys throw. There is a lot of respect—"

"Ugh, stop. Next," Torian interjected.

Marietta was cut off quickly. The next girl got up and expressed how much she liked the colors. The girl after her talked about the Bee-goh-p call. This simply had to be a joke.

"If you don't have anything meaningful to tell us, y'all need to walk out right now," Torian said as her adviser got on her for obviously being mean-spirited. "I'm just saying, give us an answer of substance."

Alyx looked directly at me. She lifted her hand in an

upward motion. I knew she wanted me to speak because I knew my stuff. My passion for this organization was real, and she could tell. I hadn't come here because of them. I had come here because I wanted to be a part of the ongoing history.

So I boldly stood. "Hi, my name is Cassidy Cross, and I would be honored and humbled to be a member of Beta Gamma Pi sorority. Though I come from humble beginnings, the Betas intervened, and they practically raised and shaped me. My mom was never around because she worked all the time, and I was always home with my uncle and my aunt. My aunt was more like my sister, at just a few years older than me. If it weren't for the Betas telling me I could be more, do more, and have more, I don't even know if I'd be in school right now. For me, it's not just about wanting to be a part of this dynamic group because of the colors, parties, and letters—I want to be a Beta because I can help expand the founders' mission. I strongly believe in the principles Beta Gamma Pi stands on: leadership, education, sisterhood—"

"Okay, okay. You know your stuff," Torian said. "Some of y'all need to wise up and learn a lesson from her."

The Betas who had been so hard on me were sending positive and approving looks my way. As soon as the rush was over, Sam and her crew asked when we could chill. I didn't answer them and just kept walking. Yeah, we might be on the line together, but I wasn't fake or phony. I certainly wasn't gonna act like we were going to be best friends because I knew more about the organization they wanted to be a part of. I was not an airhead. Yeah, I might've once been wild, but I had substance.

Instead of looking down their noses at other folks, those girls needed to do their own research. I was not a library, and I was not going to help them gain the knowledge they lacked.

"I'd like to get with you guys, too," said the girl who had been sitting alone.

"Please! We didn't even ask you," Cheryl said.

"Here. Take my number and give me a call," I said to the girl when I saw her dramatically tear up after being dissed by Sam and her crew.

When I smiled at her, I knew I'd given the girl hope. I looked over at Sam, and she couldn't even look me in the eye. She knew she and her friends were trifling. I walked away knowing I had helped make someone's day. Being a part of the solution and not the problem made me feel good.

It didn't take the girl any time to give me a call. We got together the very next day. She told me her name was Isha, and she was a junior as well. We met over breakfast and found we had some of the same classes. The day after that we got together for a study session for our psychology class.

A week later, I'd come to the conclusion that she was cool. The only quirk I found was that she was really, really into God. I found out the object she had been twirling when I'd first seen her was a cross she'd had for ten years. Every other conversation we had was about God this or our Savior that. She'd been bugging me since I met her to go to church with her.

Friday night while Sam was getting ready to go out

with her crew to a Beta jam at a school up the way, I decided I needed something, and maybe church was it. So as Isha kept asking I finally gave in. She called it a seeker-style service.

"I don't wanna sound ignorant or anything, but what's a seeker-style service? What do they do different?" I asked on the way there.

Excitedly, she raved, "Oooo, great question. The style is not boring. It's gonna be cool. The setting is like a theater, and the service is set up like a play. You'll get the message that God loves you, and He sent His only Son to die for your sins. It's not gonna be pushy, and our youth pastor is so good you'll be ready to give your heart to God. I know you're supposed to be here tonight, Cassidy. I can feel it."

I knew that was far-fetched. How in the world was a service or sermon going to make me think there was someone up there? My upbringing had been so hard. Some days there'd been no food, and there'd always been tons of pain seeing my mother sad most of the days—I just knew a God who was supposed to love me could not allow us to suffer so.

An hour later as I sat in the dark theater that didn't look like a church, I saw a skit of a girl getting raped by the most popular guy in high school. It was like déjà vu all over again. The same character wanted to commit suicide, and an angel came down from the top curtain, signifying Heaven, I guess, and told her she was worthy.

Isha was right. I was supposed to be there at that moment because something came over me, and I felt so different. I felt that even though Sam and I were disconnected, if I reflected back, she had prayed for me. Maybe just like the character on stage, God had given me another chance. I tried not to get emotional, but as Isha had verbalized, a fine young pastor—in his early twenties and about six feet with a nice frame—started talking.

"Did you see that broken young lady? Did you witness a true miracle of the Lord? This young lady gave herself to God, and He forgave her sins."

I just fell to my knees; I felt too different. His words had touched me enough to give me hope. My mom wasn't there to love me, and I had never known my dad. There were some things in my past that had hurt me so bad I had blocked them out. And to be so young and go through so much, I guess I had just never thought God was real. In my darkest hour, God had seen me through.

"Is there anybody out there who wants to be renewed?" Pastor Konner Black preached. "Or wants to be healed? Come on down right now and let the Lord give you reason to go on and a reason to wake up tomorrow."

I rose to my feet and made my way down the aisle to the altar with a heavy heart. I finally understood that though I couldn't see a God up there, He was present. And only in Him could I be fulfilled and truly have purpose.

BARRIER

"I'm tired of us walking around not speaking to each other," Sam said to me when I was studying for a test. "The tension is weighing me down, Cass."

Angrily, I threw down my pen, stopped doing my homework, and said, "That's your choice. I've never changed. I've been the same way with you. You got with your little friends and decided I wasn't worthy of your time. The problem is you never took into account that we had something tight. They might not like my style, they might think I'm a little too wild, but you know everything I've been through. Particularly lately, Samantha. And I guess I just never thought you'd throw all that away just to please girls who are so fickle. Watch yourself, or they'll be throwing you to the curb."

"Will we ever be able to get past it?" she asked me with eyes that held mine.

I knew she used to be sincere. Honestly now, though, I didn't know if she was just coming to me because, out of all of us who had attended rush last week, I was the only one who really knew my stuff. Now that the Betas didn't deem me as having the party-girl mentality, she wanted to be attached to me. It just seemed too coincidental, too fake, and too phony. I wasn't going to fall for it and then have her dump me when her crew decided to tell her to again.

I grabbed my books, shook my head, went to my room, and shut the door. However, I instantly felt uneasy about being too blunt. I really felt my heart weighing on me like I had a conscience, which was new for me because this whole Christianity thing was still in its infancy stage, as far as I was concerned. I didn't want to hurt her feelings and not take her word. If God could forgive me for all my crazy ways, I was supposed to be able to do the same. I was only human, but I had capacity to forgive. How could God be pleased with my sorry actions?

So I dropped to my knees and prayed, "Lord, all this is new for me. I'm sorry I'm not as sweet as I need to be. Help me, but right now I just can't trust her."

"There were two letters in the mail!" Sam rushed up and said five days after we'd turned in our sorority packets and had our interviews.

I didn't know Beta Gamma Pi protocol, so whether the letters meant something good, something bad, or could go either way, I had no idea. I mean, they'd never told us we were getting a phone call. Since rush, after we'd met their adviser who had told us to come to her with any drama, the Betas had actually been trying to keep as much distance as possible.

Sam and I weren't as rude to each other anymore. The smart little comments, keeping our things labeled in the refrigerator, or staying longer in the bathroom to irritate the other were dismissed over the last days. However, we were not tight, either. So whatever was in my envelope was my business. Whatever was in hers, she could share if she wanted, but I wasn't going to pry.

"Thanks, you can hand that to me," I said to her, extending my hand as I waited for the envelope addressed to Cassidy Cross.

"You don't want to open them together?" she asked as her body jumped nervously. "I've really been praying about us working through our differences. I do care a lot for you. Cassidy, please give me another chance."

"Fine," I said sarcastically, and I vented even more. "I don't know how we went wrong, where we veered off. Oh! I guess I do know, you let other people—"

"I know, I know, I know," Sam said. "I'm sorry. I know you and I don't think alike, but we do live together. It's not just because I have to get along with you that I want us to reconnect, it's because I miss you. I want our sisterhood back."

She reached out to hug me. I had to dig deep then, and I realized I did miss her as well. As far as I knew, she hadn't put my business out in the street, so even though we'd had turmoil, she had still remained somewhat loyal. Sam was a great girl, and I was a better person with her as my friend, not my foe. I hugged her.

Holding me tight, she said, "Thank you, Cass. Thanks for forgiving me."

"Thank you for saving me," I said, remembering that she had cared about me when I didn't care about myself.

When we pulled apart, she handed me my letter. "Both of our letters look just alike, so let's open them together. Good thing is, I heard that if you get a letter quickly that means you have to pay your membership fee. The other people who didn't make the line receive their letters from Grand Chapter, which is going to take a little longer, so I think we both got in!"

"All right, let's open them. One, two, three," I said, and we tore open the letters together. We both skimmed, and suddenly we were jumping up and down—until I read the fine print that said a cashier's check or money order in the amount of seven hundred fifty dollars needed to be paid by midnight the next day.

I did the only thing I could do—I called some of the Betas from back home. The two who had written my recommendation letter and who had mentored me when I was younger rounded up the Alumni chapter and wired me the money that night. They didn't have to do it, but I guess because of the love and support of the sisterhood, it was no big deal. I appreciated the monetary gesture and would forever be grateful. If it weren't for them, there would be no BGP for me.

It was fall in Arkansas, and the temperature the next morning was dropping, particularly in the wee hours. I was hesitant to pull into the abandoned parking lot to give my money to the chapter, but then I saw some bright lights flash at me. I guessed it was some sort of sign that it was cool for me to park. But after all that had happened to me in the beginning of the school year, I just wasn't sure. I opened my glove compartment and put the mace in my pocket, grabbed my cell phone, and kept it in my hand, ready to dial 911 in the event of any kind of emergency. Then Torian came out of the darkness, and even with the serious look plastered on her face, I felt more at ease.

"Do you have the money?" she asked snottily. I started to say something sassy, but I knew this was a part of the pledging process. However, when she sassed up to me with her head swinging and her mouth poked out, I knew we weren't there for congratulatory remarks.

"Even though you said a few cool things at our rush, know this, little sistah, I did not vote for you. So know there is *no* love between us," Torian said as she held her hand out, waiting for me to place the envelope in it.

Not needing her to emphasize anything with me, I said, "Sure, Torian."

"No, no, you address me as Big Sister Torian Handle That, okay?"

"I'm sorry, Big Sister Torian Handle That."

"Much better. And also, let's be clear. Al Dutch and I go out. So you and he can never be caught together again. I know he likes many girls, but I'll make him see I'm the one. And until he does, I don't want my little pledgee getting in the way of my happiness."

She was trying to explain how she had changed her mind about Al Dutch, but I couldn't hear anything but that fool's name. I wanted to scream out, *"Run as far away from him as you possibly can. Trust me, he's no good. Your first instinct was right."* But she mistook the perplexed glare I gave her to be one of jealousy.

"You don't have a choice. I'm your Big Sister here, so you do what I say. He's going to be my man, and you're going to leave him alone."

"May I speak, Big Sister Torian Handle That?" I said to her. "Here's my money. And I don't want you to take this the wrong way or anything, but you're way too good for Al Dutch."

Thinking back to the pain that chump had put me through, my chest started rising, and it was hard for me to breathe. Clearly, she could tell something was wrong and that I was uncomfortable.

She touched my back and said, "Are you okay?"

"Just thinking about my time with him. I'm not okay. Just don't."

"What happened?" Torian questioned. "I don't understand."

"Just don't. . . ." I hung my head because I could say no more. She dismissed me, and I got back in my car and drove away, hoping she had gotten the message. However, I could not stress out like that again. She was a big girl, and she was warned.

Forty of us had made line, the largest line in the past ten years for the Alpha chapter. I knew it was hard to get along with one black female, but being connected to thirty-nine of them was going to be much more drama. Sam didn't even ask me if it was okay with me to hold a meeting at our place—she just volunteered us. She started tidying up and making popcorn, and, like clockwork, they all showed up at seven PM on the dot.

Cheryl, Sam's crazy friend, was there. She was an okay-looking girl—about 5'6" with shoulder-length jet-black hair, and I noticed she had a cute smile, despite her yellow teeth. Her beauty was average, but she had really hard angles, like she was in the army or something. I confirmed my thoughts when her smile quickly changed to a tight pout and she opened her mouth to speak.

"We don't want to be paper, you guys. We want to do this thing right. All we got to do is get in the car and be with the other lines getting hazed. I heard that they are hazing a line at a school an hour away. We can go and meet up with them. If you got a test to study for, bring your materials with you. We need to be as well rounded as we can. Some of our Big Sisters may be there."

"Man, we need to hurry up!" another one of Sam's friends shouted out.

"That's really what the meeting is about. It's time for us to come together so we can be as one," Cheryl sort of demanded, motioning toward the door. "Y'all ready? Let's be out!"

Sam didn't seem to be surprised by any of this, but it was all new to me. Somebody was telling me we needed to come together and go let somebody bash our brains in, all so we wouldn't be paper? I wasn't going nowhere.

"Says who?" I yelled out.

I looked around. About half the crew had smiles on their faces, slapping each other high fives, ready to mobilize in cars and go join in other underground lines. Isha came over to me and tugged me.

"Can I speak to you for a second?" Isha said. We stepped into my bedroom. "Are you okay with this?" she asked before I could even ask her what was up.

Clearly, she could tell that I was not happy. "I mean, we just can't let them decide we're going to do something that could jeopardize all of us getting our letters. We signed a slip of paper saying we wouldn't be hazed at all. I don't know about you, Isha, but my word is my word."

She leaned in and said, "I don't want to do it."

Instantly, I was confused. "If you don't want to do it, why don't you just tell them you don't want to go out like that?"

"Come on, Cassidy, be real. They already think I'm the little Christian girl. I roll by myself all the time. That's one of the joys in wanting to be in a sorority—so I could feel important, think I had it going on. Deep down inside I don't want to be ostracized, and I could tell on some of the faces of other girls in there that everybody wasn't for it. We just need somebody who can stand up to Cheryl to say we're not doing this because our line can't be divided. Will you speak for us?"

Understanding her pleas, I nodded. I stepped out into the hall and saw Sam grabbing her purse.

"Wait a minute. We haven't finished talking about all this," I said loudly.

"We don't have a lot of time to talk about anything. We got to get in the cars and go. How many people are driving? We need to take as few vehicles as possible," Cheryl said, talking over me as if I didn't matter and as if what only she had to say counted.

I nudged my roommate. "Sam, you might want to check your girl. I just said we're not through talking."

"All right, well, calm down, Cassidy," Sam said, standing between the two of us.

"All right, you got everybody's attention. We'll be late and get in trouble with the Big Sisters down there, but what do you have to say? Cassidy, we know if they ask us any history to throw you out there because you know everything. What else you want to say?" Cheryl rudely asked.

"We haven't voted on going. I'm not for this little-go-get-hazed-by-some-sorors-who-aren't-even-in-school-at-Western-Smith bull."

"Wait, what are you saying?" Sam said to me. "You don't want to be legitimate?"

I said, "I don't know how many of you guys are for it, but everybody needs to really think about the repercussions of us stepping out there and somebody getting hurt, us getting caught, or who knows whatever else."

Isha yelled out, "We could go to jail!"

"We could get thrown out of school," said somebody else who was on our side.

"Oh, what, so half of y'all don't want to go?" Cheryl said. "Sam, you need to check your roommate. All those who are ready, let's roll out."

Sam turned and walked toward the door. I grabbed her arm. She needed to rethink following a nut because she was on her way to getting cracked. I pleaded, "Don't do this."

"Sam, let's go!" Cheryl called, almost screaming.

Half of the sorors were out the door; the other half of us were inside with arms folded, clearly not moving. Sam was torn. Before our line had officially been inducted as initiates to the Beta Gamma Pi pledge process, we were already divided. There Sam stood between right and wrong.

GLORIOUS

I leaned over to Samantha as we stood in the middle of our line sisters, anxiously knowing that whatever we decided was going to affect everyone. "Before you head out of here, you really need to make sure you're okay with risking all of us not being Betas. Maybe we should just take a second and really think about the repercussions of all this," I said to Sam.

She looked over at Cheryl with eyes that longed for compromise. The girls who stood behind me sat on the floor. This bold move spoke volumes. Until we truly discussed this, all of us were not going.

Sam and Cheryl whispered stuff to each other. The girls outside started having doubtful faces. Sensing she was losing the argument, Cheryl called everyone back into the apartment.

"Can you at least tell us how this all came about?" I

asked Cheryl, trying to keep my cool with the chick I felt was a head case.

"Come on, Cass. We all have friends who go to different schools. My home girl I went to high school with is on the line up there, and if we want any respect we're supposed to go up there and see them along with two other lines. We're already late."

I began my rounds of serious, thought-provoking questions. "Doesn't that seem odd to you? We're not even officially on line, yet we got to come there right now or they're going to deem us paper? That just seems strange to me. Don't you think we should talk to one of our own Big Sisters to find out if that's what we should really do? You mentioned some of Alpha chapter may be there, Cheryl—do you know if they will be there for sure? Honestly, they could hate the fact that we went without being told to."

"But if you talk to one of them, they're not going to let us go. Going through other Beta chapters keeps them from being directly involved. Plus, you know Dr. Garnes has them on a tight leash. So what if they don't go or don't know? We still want Betas everywhere to give us props. Come on, you guys. We pay now and get much respect later." Cheryl looked around, waiting for everyone to feel her argument. "Everybody doing this is legitimate. Our Big Sisters went through a lot. We've all heard the stories. They get much admiration not only because they're Alpha chapter but . . . I can't even say it. You know why they get mad respect."

I attempted to reason. "Yeah, I know why, because

somebody lost their life during their pledge process. And we should be standing in line, getting in our cars, jumping up and down, ready to follow that crazy path? Man, that is just foolishness to me. I'm not doing it. You all can go ahead and call me whatever you want—paper, napkin, towel . . ."

Many started laughing. I was serious though. Cheryl made the meanest face. The majority of us didn't care about her tantrum.

I wanted to be part of a sisterhood, not a zoo. I could think for myself, and I could rationalize right from wrong. A part of being on a line was to develop unity, to find one voice, to put a whole bunch of different opinions under a microscope and come out with a plan. But even if we all didn't agree, we still supported the majority. And although that was the sister theory, where was I going to draw the line? When would I stand up for what was right? Would I go along even if that meant someone else dying?

Thinking about trying to please everyone, I stood and said, "Look, I'm not trying to be popular here, and I'm not trying to cause problems. I just want to stand for what I think is right for all of us. I got a pretty good relationship with the leader of our line. I'm going to call Alyx and see what she thinks about this whole thing. If she thinks we should do it, I'll go. That's the best I can tell you."

"So you're going to jeopardize us to get your own piece of mind? What if she says no and then you won't go and our line is divided?" Cheryl said, not budging from her point of view.

"Well, if she's the leader of the line you're signing up to be on, and she says no, you shouldn't want to go, and our line will be one," I retorted.

Sam pulled Cheryl over to the side when she got up in my face and I didn't back down by standing straight up in hers. I was doing all I could to compromise, and they had to do the same. As much as I wanted to stick to my former outburst and not go, I was open to doing what Alyx said.

I overheard Sam say, "That's reasonable, Cheryl. Come on. Cass is more than trying."

Isha was behind my back and egging me on, saying, "That's right, you told her right."

Cheryl came over to me and said, "Make the call." Everybody sat down when I called Alyx.

"Put me on loudspeaker or something. I need to talk to everybody, and I can't come over there and see y'all because that is against our rules," Alyx said as I followed her instructions and hit the button. "Hey, y'all, this is Alyx." Everybody said hey. "Just so we have an understanding, there are going to be some of my sorors who may try to get you guys to do this and that, participating in all kinds of stuff, and as long as you guys are going through Alpha chapter, know for sure you will be legit. But we need you to trust us and do it our way, so if you're not down with that whole plan, maybe you need to rethink whether you should pledge before we have the meeting completing this pledge process tomorrow. So no going down to another school, got it?" She hung up the phone.

We all just sat there, each and every person deciding

for themselves if and why they wanted to be a part of Alpha chapter. Though everyone wasn't pleased, we all collectively agreed, even Cheryl, that we weren't going to go get hazed. We were one.

We'd officially been on line for two weeks now. We'd been inducted as Pis, we were bonding as a group, and we'd been through three different ceremonies. Each was getting us a step closer to hopefully becoming full members of the best sorority around. We actually had two lines. One in which we lined up in alphabetical order— because lining up by height was considered a form of hazing—and one in which we ignored the rule and lined up by height anyway (when we weren't in the presence of Alumni chapter members, Dr. Garnes, or anyone from the campus). I wasn't the tallest person, so I was number three of forty.

"You know what tonight's ceremony is about?" Isha, who happened to be number four, asked me. "I'm so excited!"

We'd gone through Gem one, a seminar on leadership, learning that every member of Beta Gamma Pi stands for excellence and is a pioneer. Gem two was about sisterhood; the basic principle we got from that special night was that we were joining a sorority. We each had our own family, but we were now joining a new family of incredibly strong sisters. The Gem targeted how you should care about others as you cared about yourself and that you should never intentionally break that rule. Gem three was about education; Betas were smart because we always knew there was more we could learn. Now we were headed to Gem ceremony number four. Yeah, I knew what it was on: Christianity. Because I was a new believer, I was a little less enthusiastic. The President of the chapter, Malloy, and Alyx came into the large dressing room of the school's historic theater, which was where the ceremony was being held, and addressed us.

Malloy, with a stern face, spoke first. "Listen up, y'all. I'm just going to be honest. My mother's the National President, so I get to preview a lot of information that the Grand Chapter gives about all the chapters. Also, because my mother doesn't want me to let her down and be the one to blame if this chapter happens to get taken for good, I'm just going to keep it real and let everyone know I'm not going to allow anybody to jeopardize Alpha chapter."

Isha elbowed me and whispered, "What's going on now? What did we miss?"

"We've been informed," Alyx said, equally perturbed, "that a few of you guys have been participating with the underground line at another collegiate chapter."

My heart started racing because Sam and I were cool. But now that I thought about it, I hadn't seen her around the house lately, and I hadn't been drilling her about what she was doing, because we only had a limited amount of time to study and get work done before it was time to participate in pledge activities. Certainly, she hadn't gone and gotten herself involved in something that jeopardized her dream of being in the best sorority in the world.

Malloy continued, "I see y'all looking all around. If you guys want to come forward and spill if you've been participating, that's fine. But just so you know, I do have pictures."

Though I didn't want to see anybody go, I had to be honest, it was a great moment when Sam said, "See, I told you all not to go down there."

Some girls in the middle of the line just stood there like they didn't know who she was talking to. I knew Cheryl was one of them.

However, Cherly shocked me when she stood beside Sam and said, "We decided we weren't going to go. It was all of us or none of us. We decided we weren't supposed to go, and I told you three to stick with us and not go out like that. Dang, y'all."

Three girls got out of line and followed Malloy out of the room. Sam started crying. The other three girls were part of her crew. Now it seemed they were out.

Alyx addressed us. "I'm glad it was just three of you guys. I'd hate to lose our whole line because you couldn't follow our rules. We're founded on Christian principles, and tonight's Gem is so important to me because God saved my life, turned my life around, and has given me a new hope. I learned that if you do things the right way, the way the Bible tells you to, everything will work out. As you go through this Gem ceremony tonight, remember those three sisters who just left. They couldn't obey the plan and they will suffer the consequences for it. When you follow His plan for your life, you can truly have happiness."

Dr. Garnes was leading the ceremony. We were standing on a piece of purple carpet they had brought in that signified the royalty of the king. We held up our right hands and read the oath on the card in front of us. We followed Dr. Garnes's words.

"I vow to keep the Lord in my heart and to always let his life shine in me, allowing the Holy Spirit to make me the best Beta I can be," Dr. Garnes said. "As I touch each of your heads with a drop of this anointed oil, I pray that you take time to take in God's word, understand his purpose and plan for your life, and, above all, strive to please him."

I realized at that moment that I couldn't be a Beta if I didn't believe in God. The Christian principles and the sorority's mission were one and the same. We learned that day that the only thing that held Beta Gamma Pi together wasn't the sisters but the love of Christ that connected all our hearts. Part of the ceremony also had to do with Jesus dying on the cross. The correlation was made between that and giving our life to public service—that we should do it with Jesus in the forefront of our brains, remembering that we would lay it all out to help another. Going through that ordeal with Al Dutch had broken me, and a part of my humanity had been taken. However, going through the ceremony and losing myself in the flame, I felt a passion for Christ. I was able to feel again, care again, want again, dream again, and hope again.

Malloy closed the ceremony by saying, "All our Gems mean something special, but this Gem is particularly meaningful because without Christ we can do nothing. With Him all things are possible. I encourage each of you Pis to dig deep within your soul, and as you look at that flame you've lit, recommit yourself to God. But as you extinguish the flame, know that you're loved by God, and anything preventing you from fully giving your heart will fade away with the smoke."

When the ceremony was over, a lot of us were in tears, including me. We were all encouraged to go home and study for the upcoming Beta Gamma Pi test we had to pass in order to move on to the next Gem. There was one more ceremony to go through tomorrow, dealing with public service, but for now we were dismissed.

Isha came over to me and asked if I wanted to help out at her church. I was sort of tired, but it was Halloween, and a lot of the Pis couldn't go to the parties because we had to lay low. I didn't want to just sit home because I knew Sam was going to have some of the girls who were dismissed off line over at our place, and I wasn't feeling pity for them. Maybe church was just where I needed to be so I could pray for them and for myself.

As soon as we got there, the youth pastor, Konner Black—the one who had made me realize I needed to let God into my life—stood right there in front of me. He had been handsome onstage, but he was even cuter just inches away. I was really digging him.

"Hi, you're Isha's friend, right?" he asked, smiling at me.

"Yes," I said, thinking he may be feeling me as well.

"I'm Konner, a new pastor here. I remember when you accepted the Lord a couple months ago. I haven't seen you back here since. Isha told me y'all are pledging," he said awkwardly.

"Yeah, I know who you are, but you say that like you have problems with the sororities or something."

"No, I'm just saying Greek life does a lot of good for the community, but a lot of people misuse the letters and end up doing more harm than good. But I don't know. I'm looking at you right now, and you got this glow about you. Halloween night, and you're in a church. I hope you and Isha do cross. I know you'll both make this world a better place through the sorority and on your own," he said in a sweeter tone, realizing he may have unintentionally offended me.

Calmer, I said, "I hope so. I'm new at this Christian thing, but it's real to me. I feel different, and I don't want to mess up or to have my heart go back to the way it used to be. I don't want to let God down, and maybe that's why I'm here tonight. I'm staying connected with the Lord and just talking to Him."

"Reading the Word and being with other believers is definitely a step in the right direction. We all fall short—keep that in mind. God's not asking you to be perfect but to have a heart that wants to please Him," he said as his mesmerizing dark brown eyes held mine. He reached over and touched my cheek. My knees felt weak. He just seemed too good to be true. Surely too nice to be into me.

I found a way to smile and not take it all so seriously. I didn't know how we were connecting in that moment, but we were. After Al Dutch, I didn't think I'd feel anything for a male again. But just to have Konner listen and point me back to God impacted me greatly and made me feel glorious.

6

PITIFUL

Konner had a unique way of ministering to young adults. It was Halloween night. People were dressed up as their favorite characters, idols, and celebrities. In stark contrast, his sermon was about how fake and unreal we are with God and how we sometimes try to mask and hide what is going on with us instead of being authentic and letting it all out to the Man above.

He preached, "If you really wanna get close to the Lord and grow in your walk with God, give Him all that's weighing you down so that you can be free to soar and be about His business. The baggage and hurt that we carry stick so deep in our minds that we don't even realize how it's hindering us from being used by the Lord."

Just as the first skit about the girl who'd been raped had moved me and mirrored my situation, I braced myself as I watched another powerful drama. Only this time the skit involved a male—a male who was going through a scene in which he just couldn't remember what had happened to him. Why was he so distant? Why couldn't he love? And why couldn't he give God his all? When the choir came on and sang the song of healing, I just knew God was speaking to my soul.

Later on that night when I went home, I had some real soul-searching to do. I got down on my knees, and I silently prayed, *Lord, there's a lot in my past that has led me to a life full of turmoil and sin. And to get stronger and to deal with it, I just sort of partied my cares away. I'm ready to love You with my whole heart, but something is holding me back. Help me to dig deep and find out what it is. I'm pledging a sorority, but I'm still a little cold to the other girls. I just need Your help, Lord. I just need Your assistance to learn what I may have gone through that has made me this way.*

Over the next three nights, God heard my plea because He showed up in my dreams and made me unable to sleep. I kept seeing images of a little girl in a closet with an older man. I couldn't see faces. I couldn't see body parts. I could see only darkness. Why did it hurt so badly?

We had one more Gem ceremony to go, and I was supposed to be there. However, when I realized that the little girl in the images was me and over the years I had blocked out something so bad, I just started shaking all over. I was so angry! I was confused as to who the man was. Was it one of my mom's boyfriends who had abused me? Was I abused by a stranger? Until I sorted all this out, I couldn't move. I had to deal with my demons and face the truth.

I thought I heard Sam banging on my door for me to come out so we could head over to the ceremony. However, I placed a pillow over my head and tried to block out the irritating noise. If the Betas dropped me, so be it, but in my frail state I would be no good to them if I went. I didn't think I was crazy, I just felt like I was strung out on drugs or something.

I couldn't help but cry out, "Lord, you're supposed to help! This hurts too badly. Why can't I make out what happened? With You by my side I can handle anything, right? Then help me. Please, Father."

My forehead and body were exploding with sweat. I lifted up the window to catch a breeze. As the day turned into the night, I desperately needed to seek out answers.

"Cassidy, you're just a trip, only caring about yourself. You do whatever you wanna do, coming to practice when you please. You tell all of us we have to be there, and you don't even show up. We know you're on line, but homecoming is coming up, and we don't wanna do the same ol' routine," Ginger whined into the answering machine as I half listened, still in a dazed state.

Whatever she was saying didn't phase me. It certainly didn't move me to pick up the phone for her. As much as the band meant to me, I couldn't deal with them right now.

Her voice continued into the machine. "If you don't get down here I'm going to teach the routine, and I'm going to tell the band director—"

The paused intrigued me, yet I was so weak I couldn't make out what was happening. All of a sudden I heard noises inside my place, and I thought I heard Sam's voice coming through the machine. "Ginger, wait, wait. This is her roommate, Sam. She hasn't been with us, and I was hoping she was at band practice."

Next thing I knew, Isha was standing in my face with a straightened-out hanger in her hand. I guess she'd picked my lock. Sam was right next to her holding our phone as Ginger continued carrying on.

"She's in here!" Isha called out.

I was so down and depressed I was having an out-of-body experience. My room was filled with my line sisters, yet I still felt like I was all alone. Isha lifted my head, and when she let go, it fell again.

"Unless she's in the hospital," Ginger's voice continued through the receiver, "I'm reporting her, and she's gonna lose her position as captain. He might just kick her off the team altogether. Ain't nothing wrong with her. And if it is, what have y'all Pis been letting the Betas do to you guys anyway? Something illegal?"

"Okay, that's it. This chick is starting to get on my last nerve. All in our business and stuff," Cheryl said, frustrated with Ginger's attitude. Cheryl bent down, and tears started coming from her eyes. I must have been in bad shape for Cheryl to break down like this. When I didn't respond, Cheryl said, "Come on, Cassidy. So many people need you. What's wrong, girl?"

Isha said, "I just don't like this, you guys."

Cheryl grabbed my arm and quickly let it go. "Man, she's completely cold. Looks like she hasn't bathed either.

Shut that window. She's freezing. Pis, we gotta help our line sister."

I felt covers around me and someone touching my feet. I felt so much care and concern, but I was too far gone to appreciate it. What was wrong with me?

"Oh! It stinks in here, guys. Look at the mess she's made. We gotta get her to the tub," Isha said when the covers on my bed were peeled back.

"Hold on, now. I ain't doing all that," Cheryl said.

"Well, I'll help clean her up," Isha volunteered.

When they lifted me up I didn't make a fuss. I didn't say stop, leave me alone, get out. Nothing. I was still stuck in a daze. I wasn't drugged up, but again, it sure did feel like I was on some weird high or low.

An hour went by. I was clean and dry, and I was staring at a fresh bowl of chicken noodle soup in front of me. Bad as my stomach wanted it, my hands just couldn't lift the spoon to feed myself.

"Y'all think she's on drugs?" Sam asked in a caring tone.

"This is really scary," Isha said as she walked over and wrapped her arms around my neck. "Come on, Cassidy. Please talk to us and tell us what's wrong."

How could I tell them what was wrong when I didn't know myself? We had lost three line sisters, and we were desperately trying to bond. I was an only child, and I longed for sisterhood so I could be around a family that truly cared for me. I sat there unable to communicate with them—to reach out and thank them for not giving up on me.

Cheryl, in particular, was being very motherly. When I

wasn't eating, she was practically forcing the fluids down my throat. The girls were getting on her about making certain I did not choke. Cheryl replied, "Don't worry. I got this. We're gonna get her well. Something traumatic has caused her to freak out like this. She needs us."

"Should we call the paramedics? The police? We can't keep letting her respond to us like this. What if somebody really did give her something? What if she's in pain?" Isha asked, pacing tensely around the place.

When I saw two tears slowly drop, one from Isha and one from Sam, I uttered, "I'm okay."

I spoke in such a whisper they couldn't even hear what I said. They knew I was saying something. And though I gave only a small response, I knew my line sisters were grateful. As Cheryl held my hand, I felt thankful. Someway, somehow we were going to figure out my issues together.

After eating the whole bowl of soup, I felt better. Physically, at least. Mentally, I was still very torn. Emotionally, I was ecstatic to have my line sisters surrounding me in the apartment I shared with Sam. Thank goodness it was clean. But inwardly I was still struggling with a lot.

The nonsense that had happened at the beginning of the school year with Al Dutch had taken such a terrible toll on me I hadn't even realized how fragile and unwound I truly was. Though I longed to forget the terrible attack, my mind kept bringing back remnants of it. Feeling like my head was gonna explode, I was completely overwhelmed.

"What about our chapter adviser? If you don't talk to us, Cassidy, will you talk to Dr. Garnes? She's a psychiatrist. She could really help you." I could not give Isha an answer either way.

Cheryl took Isha by the arm and dragged her to the other side of the room. The two were conversing as if I weren't there. Actually, I guess I wasn't there.

"Girl, she doesn't need to see a shrink! I know what's going on. She lost her boyfriend," Cheryl said, thinking she had my issues pegged.

"What? What do you mean she lost her boyfriend?" Isha asked with a shriveled-up face, not believing Cheryl knew what she was talking about.

Cheryl confessed, "She was dating Al Dutch, but he's with me now. That's right, when I leave from pledging with y'all, I'm with him. Things are getting really intense between us."

I picked up the now empty soup bowl and threw it across the room. I was beyond shocked. I mean, come on. If it wasn't me, it was Ginger, Meagan, Torian, and now Cheryl. This guy was going to keep up his dirty work of scrambling through us women unless I said something. And if he did to them what he did to me and I kept quiet, I couldn't live with myself.

Cheryl began pacing back and forth. "See, I knew that's what it was. Sam, did you tell her I was with Al? That's what's going on with her. You must've blabbed."

"I didn't say anything," Sam defended. "Why would I tell Cassidy? I told you Al Dutch needs to be left alone."

The two of them started arguing. I knew Sam wanted

to tell Cheryl more about Al Dutch but could not because she was keeping my confidence. With my hands to my face, I started crying.

"It's hot," I said in a weak tone.

Sam cleared everyone out of the apartment. Without even knowing it, I was rocking back and forth, and Isha helped me over to our cozy sofa. Cheryl wanted to stay because she felt responsible. And I didn't want her to go. I needed to get some information to her, but the words wouldn't come out. What was going on with me that allowed me to punk out?

Somehow someone got in touch with Dr. Garnes because she was ushered into the apartment with Sam, heading straight toward me. I didn't want to end up in some mental hospital with padded walls and straitjackets, but something was deeply wrong. I was so upset, so confused, so depressed, so down I was doing things I didn't know I was capable of. If a shrink or medical help could bring me back around, bring it on.

"I don't like making house calls like this: seeing patients at home can sometimes be tricky. I don't wanna lose my license, but to you girls my attention is immediately given, being that I am the adviser for this chapter. So, Sam, I'm going to ask you to be a witness, and if you feel that Cassidy is uncomfortable, you make the call to stop this session. Cassidy, it's Dr. Garnes. Would you like to talk to me?" she asked, and I nodded. "Good. I'm going to ask Sam to fix you some herbal tea. Because you're already sitting on the couch, I'm going to ask you to lie down. Sam, I'm also going to need a washcloth, and make it hot."

After drinking the hot tea and relaxing, I felt like I was in some sauna at the spa. It took Dr. Garnes forty-five minutes to get me to respond to her. When I finally opened up, I just let it all hang out.

Exhilarated, I spilled one deep word after another. "Something happened to me when I was a child. Either I don't remember, or I don't wanna remember, but it just surfaced to me, and it's making me go bonkers. I mean, one minute I'm lucid, and the next minute I'm totally insane. I need help badly. I'm so sorry I made it hard for my line sisters."

"Cassidy, it's okay. You didn't make it hard for anybody. Tell me what's been going on. We need to figure all this out," Dr. Garnes said as she took notes.

Grabbing her sleeve, I said, "I need you to keep this to yourself."

"Would you like for Sam, Isha, and Cheryl to leave?" Dr. Garnes asked, assuming I needed privacy.

"No, she can stay, but I need this not to be repeated." Dr. Garnes nodded and gave me the assurance that talking would help. "A couple months ago I was raped. I think one of my mom's boyfriends raped me when I was young, too. The memories of both horrible events keep plaguing my brain. I don't know how to deal with all this. I feel so sorry for myself right now. I'm pitiful."

7

BOUNCE

A week later, I was back at dance practice in stride again. Although Ginger had made up the moves and thought they would be too difficult for me to learn at the eleventh hour, I was throwing down on her dance that I had to admit was pretty tight. Before practice started, however, we had a lot of drama. She had gone to the band director to get him to agree not to let me be in the homecoming festivities because I had missed so many practices.

Thankfully, Director Paxton had my back and was fine with the fact that I had been incapacitated. Dr. Garnes had written me a doctor's note and had worked with me consistently over the last week. She had even put me on some meds and, thankfully, though I couldn't say I was back to my old self, I was vibrant, fun, and not taking it all so seriously.

Though it would have been nice to have had friends on the dance team, I knew that was impossible. Having buddies in this group was a waste because folks wished I wasn't the team captain. I knew a lot of the jealousy toward me spawned from Ginger and Meagan as a result of Al Dutch. They had issues with each other as well. I'm sure when I had been gone they had had their power struggle over who would rule. Though Ginger had won, and now everyone including Meagan was following her lead, I knew they wanted it to stay that way. So instead of trying to create more havoc and demand their respect, I went over to Ginger and tried to make peace.

"Can I please talk to you for a sec? I just need a bit of your time," I said to her after practice when everyone else was dismissed.

"Yeah, what do you want?" Ginger said with severe attitude.

Ignoring her snobbish retort, I said, "I just wanted to let you know I really like your dance. Girl, it is hot. We're gonna turn a lot of heads with that smooth groove at homecoming."

"You think so?" she said, absolutely blown away that I was giving her accolades.

I could tell I had swept her off her feet with my response. I wasn't being fake and phony about it. Making up hot dances wasn't easy, so if I saw someone who had skills, she needed to be told so. That was the drum-major side of me coming out. Director Paxton had told me that encouraging section leaders only made for a healthy, more whole, happier band.

I nodded. "Yes, I'm serious, I like it."

She didn't know how to respond. We had been playing tit for tat all year long. She'd say something mean to me; I would say something mean back to her. We needed to cut all that out. The same day she'd tried unsuccessfully to get me kicked off the team indefinitely and created a big mess was the same day I had realized the feud had to end. It was a big move on my part, and I set myself up so she could make me eat crow or make me glad I showed class and extended an olive branch.

Thankfully, she chose the latter when she said, "I can't believe you liked it. To have your approval really is an honor. No one has hooked us up like you. The whole school likes our halftime performances. None of us tell you, but we get stopped after games by people asking us who choreographed the number. You come up with the best moves around. To have your approval is a big deal, and you inspired some of the moves. You really like it, Cassidy?"

Happy to hear her tell me that folks liked my numbers as well, I remembered this was about her and said, "I really like it. Of course I wanted to be able to come to those practices, but I had some other stuff going on. You stepped up to the plate and worked out a routine that's on point. My goal for the squad this year was to compete at the national dance competition on the collegiate level, and with this routine, we might be able to do that. I mean, if you're willing."

"I feel so bad," she said, hanging her head lower. "I've been jealous of you all year long. The guy I went out with wanted to be with you more than me. If he hadn't ditched me as soon as he'd laid eyes on you, it wouldn't have driven a wedge between you and me and the friendship we could have possibly had."

"I don't want Al Dutch! He's beyond a jerk," I quickly told her, knowing who she was referring to.

"I've learned the hard way I don't want to be with him ever again either. I don't even want to talk about him. Al Dutch, who?" she said, and we both laughed. "Now he's with Meagan and tons of other girls, too."

"So who cares what he does? Can you and I make some type of truce?" I reached out my hand. "I'm pledging Beta, and I'll need to lean on you to help me with the dance team."

"We're cool," she said as she reached out her hand. "And you can count on me."

"Ginger, this really means a lot. You're talented, and I take this band seriously. You lead well, and we need to show unity to make the squad know we're not divided."

"I'm with you. I just feel so free now," she said. "I came around to like you. I mean, I could really learn a lot from you. Truth be told, you gave me the inspiration for the dance I created. Thank you for being open to the idea of trying something for me when I tried to bash you. I don't deserve any kind of friendship from you. I turned the team against you. I don't know," she said, looking away.

"I guess one thing I've learned," I stepped up to her, "is that we make mistakes in this life while we're still young and in college for goodness' sake, but we're here to get smarter and not just academically. We've got a lot of life lessons to learn, and if we can move past our differences, to me it shows we've got an element of compassion inside us that could come only from a higher power."

"Believe it or not, I've been praying that I wouldn't be so mean. I guess God heard me."

"I guess God heard us both," I said as we hugged.

"So you know we were really worried about you, right?" Cheryl said to me later that night when I was with my line sisters at the bonding slumber tea hosted by the alumnae sorors. "This is supposed to be a bonding session. Couldn't think of nobody better to open it up than you, Cassidy. Can you tell us what's wrong with you, girl?"

"I don't really want anyone to worry about me. I'm okay now." Everybody was looking at me like *You better be real and tell us what was wrong with you.* "I feel like I've been tough pretty much all my life. I can't explain last week."

I had been back studying with my sisters to get ready for the Beta Gamma Pi exam we'd all have to pass to become initiated. However, no one had been bold enough to come up to me and ask what was going on. Sam had been kind enough to keep everything she knew confidential. But as I was not being that open, and as this was the time to connect, I had to face the big question. Would I open up and be vulnerable and really cut through the layers I'd held up for years? Or would I stay closed off?

Seeing faces that cared and remembering them all around my bedside when I could not speak, I humbly uttered, "I don't want you all to be mad. The truth is I

don't really know all the details about these crazy dreams
I've been having. I had some kind of meltdown, and in
some way it had to deal with my childhood not being the
best. Some things happened, and it was traumatizing,
and as much as I tried to push it aside and bury it and act
like I didn't go through what I went through, it affected
me. The horrible past I refused to remember has just
made me crazy. Thanks to your love and your kindness, I
got through this rough time. And now I want to be a Beta
more than ever. I always wanted to be one to serve the
community. At first, the whole sisterhood part I could
sort of do without, but now the oneness I feel with all of
you is heartfelt. I'm really blessed to be a part of it.
Thanks for pushing me through."

I wasn't trying to make anybody cry or be sad or anything like that, but I turned around, and a few of them
were weeping.

Number five on the line—the shy girl who never said a
word—said, "I know that y'all call me Lele, but my real
name is Kelly Reese, and I'm from Mississippi. Like Cassidy, I had a traumatic experience when I was a kid. I witnessed my dad kill my mom. I'm an only child. I lost both
my parents in one day. My dad went to prison, and my
mom was dead. I never thought I'd have any family anymore. I didn't know how to be sociable, and y'all have
opened up your hearts to me, too, and it feels so good."

Isha stood up and said, "I've been alone most of my
life ever since I accepted Jesus into my heart in the fifth
grade. I have always been like a minister. I felt like I was
supposed to proclaim his word, and that kept a lot of
people away. I guess I thought a sorority would be differ-

ent. It would give me some identity and unity. I mean, not that Christ wouldn't give me identity enough, but you know what I'm saying." We all nodded, understanding what she meant: she wanted to be cool. "I've watched this line go from being a bunch of pieces to being one complete unit in a matter of few weeks, and I knew heaven was on our side."

"But, see, I guess that's the thing," Cheryl chimed in. "I'm tired of you always talking about heaven and pleasing God and stuff. Maybe you just come across so preachy. It just makes people not want to relate."

"But I guess that's the thing I love about the line now. We are all so different. Some of us are loud, some of us are quiet, some of us are preachy, and some of us are harsh," Isha said, looking directly at Cheryl. "But just like me, you feel down and defeated sometimes. Yet despite our differences, we can come together as one unit. I think we are all making this line something dynamite. We're each contributing as we lend our own personalities to the line. Yet that crazy, weird mix is making one strong whole."

"You're right," Cheryl said as many of us nodded in agreement. "I'm sorry. Where would we be without your strong tie with the Lord?" She smiled, and we all smiled, too.

We ended up talking about some of the problems we had early on and some of the problems other lines had that we'd heard about. We vowed to keep the communication open so we would be free to love and continue to build on our relationship. The oneness was something special.

* * *

Later that night while we were sleeping, Dr. Garnes was in another room. There was a knock on our door, and we were startled when it opened up on its own. In came five of the Alpha chapter sisters. Torian grabbed the sheets and threw them off everybody. Another girl came in and started splashing water across our faces.

"Get up! Get up right now! Get up!"

Looking around for the Beta leaders, I huffed when I didn't see Malloy or Alyx anywhere—those were the two who had kept their heads on straight, not wanting to give our line any form of hazing. And to see that mean look in Torian's eyes, I knew she was up to no good. But what were we to do? We were told not to participate in hazing with some other chapter because that could jeopardize things, but if our own Big Sisters asked us, demanded that we follow them out of the room and out of the hotel into the dark night into some woods nearby, who were we to resist? If we followed them and Alpha chapter got in trouble, it wasn't on us anymore. But if we didn't go, all the collegiates in the state, in the region, and in Grand Chapter would know we were paper, and deep down neither I nor my line sisters truly wanted that.

"Listen," Torian said once we were outside in line from shortest to tallest. All thirty-seven of us were shaking in the cold night's air. "You guys need to put your hands on your sister's shoulders in front of you. Don't let anyone come between you and the person in front of you. We've got stockings we're going to put around your eyes now, and this is called a project of trust."

Isha stood behind me and said, "Okay, I'm a little scared now."

I took a couple deep breaths and wondered if I was being a punk for going along and not questioning this. Had Torian and her girls thought this through?

Apparently they hadn't, because Torian called out to one of them, "All right, Loni, I love you, girl, but I'm not going to bring on a group of girls and not have them be real. I'm just not down for it. I'm just not ready for it. I just have to put my hands on them and make them some group we can be proud of."

"But do we have to do that by whooping them?" Loni said to her.

Isha shoved me. "Did you hear that? Whooping? I can't have anyone touch me, Cass, I'll break. What are we going to do?"

"I'm thinking," I said.

We were blindfolded by that point. None of us knew if they were really going to beat us or not. All of a sudden we heard folks wrestling around. It seemed Loni and Torian were fighting and then folks were screaming out. Was it the Betas trying to mess with us, or were some of our sorors in the back of the line getting beat down? We were locked together, and we were told not to let anybody break the line, and then we felt a few people bum-rushing us. It was more than just seven. It had to be about twenty—no, thirty—no, maybe forty voices we heard around us. What in the world was going on? And how could we make this stop?

All right, Lord, we were crazy enough to go for all this,

and now it's getting out of hand. I don't know if they're messing with us or if someone is getting beat for real, but this is not cool.

And as soon as God heard my prayer, we heard Dr. Garnes's voice and could see a bright reflection shining on us. "What is going on out here? I know this isn't what I think it is! Why would you all risk your chapter forever? Everybody who doesn't go to Western Smith College better get out of here right now. Did I not speak your language? Move! Go! Bounce!"

GREAT

"Nobody's moving. Did you all think I'm playing? Betas who don't go to this school, get your stuff and get your butts out of here right now! Alpha chapter, front and center!" Dr. Garnes yelled. "Pis, take those blindfolds off. You know you signed a policy saying you wouldn't be hazed."

"Torian, I thought you had your adviser in check," said a Beta I had never seen before. On her jacket were the Greek letters for Gamma Psi, so I knew she was from another school. Torian looked like she was now very mad our adviser had gotten her punked in front of other Betas.

"Please, y'all just go," Torian said to the Gamma Psi sorors. "Sorry it didn't go down the way we planned, but I need to handle this lady. We just got her as an adviser this year, and it seems she needs to be replaced."

"Yeah, she does," the other Beta from the other school uttered, rolling her eyes at Dr. Garnes.

After we followed the orders of the adviser, Isha leaned over and whispered to me, "Weren't we supposed to take off our blindfolds? Look at Torian staring at us like we did something wrong. We had a direct order from the head lady in charge. We might not be able to even cross because we did this anyway."

We remained in one line. I could hear the heavy breathing coming from my line sisters. We were in the middle, and the middle was the hot spot. As Torian and Dr. Garnes eyed each other down, I knew things were about to get even hotter.

"And, pledges, get out of line right now!" Dr. Garnes screamed out. "You're not supposed to be hazed. You're not supposed to be feeling like you got to please these girls in order to cross over. You're supposed to go directly by the book. You must not want to become Betas."

Many of us started saying, "Yes, we do. We're sorry," and much other mumbo jumbo that let the adviser know she need not get it twisted: we did want to pledge.

"Like any of them wants to be paper, though," Loni said in a whisper, clearly also heated by Dr. Garnes.

"Did you say something?" Dr. Garnes went over to Loni with her hand on her hip.

"We're just saying we got this," Torian said bluntly.

"Do Alyx and Malloy know you're out here? I need to know how far all this deception goes. It is one thing to think it's cute and fun to have these girls out here, but it's another to think it's legitimate. Besides, all this wanting-props stuff is pure foolishness and ain't about nothing. I told you girls to fall out of line," Dr. Garnes said to us.

We all looked at Torian, and her eyes were like *Do not move. I didn't give you an order to walk anywhere.* What were we to do?

It might not even matter anyway, now that Dr. Garnes had found out. If she turned us all in, certainly we would not be able to cross. But if we ticked off our Big Sisters, would crossing without their blessing be worth it?

Torian said, "This is bull. We weren't even doing anything to these girls. You have no proof of that. We didn't tell them to put those covers on their faces. We don't even know what it is they're wearing."

"Torian, I know you don't think I'm that ignorant. These are stockings, and I'm sure if I took them down to the local police station, all of your prints would be on them and not just these girls'. So are you telling me you didn't touch any of these blindfolds?"

Torian rolled her eyes and then looked away.

Loni said to Dr. Garnes, "Can't you just, like, go back to those other old ladies and enjoy social time? We understand where you're coming from now. We won't hurt anybody."

"It was one of those old ladies who heard some commotion and noise coming from her window. We fussed and argued back and forth because I just knew there was no way you Betas would've found us and been up here messing with these girls on our alumnae weekend. Though I've only been your adviser for less than a year, I pledged this chapter more than twenty-five years ago. When the regional coordinator and state director asked me to take this post, I assured them in no way was I going to tolerate any foolishness from you all. Be clear, I will not lose my letters trying to help you all save yours from any wrongdoing on your part. If any of this gets out that I found out and didn't report it, it'll all be on me." She turned and looked at us one more time. "I don't know why y'all are scared to move, but I told you to go! I'll let you know in the morning what my decision is going to be—don't make me make it right here and now. Trust me, none of you wants me to use my cell phone and report this one. But if these pledges don't get back inside right now, pack their bags, and head home, I will." Dr. Garnes held her cell high.

"Let's jet, Pis!" I screamed out, making the call.

Cheryl looked at me and nodded. "Yeah, let's go."

When the thirty-seven of us got back to the room, we packed up our stuff. All of us were breathing hard, extremely nervous, palms sweating, and some of us weren't able to breathe. What we'd done was severe. Had we messed up our chance? What was going to happen to Torian and Loni and the other Betas with us? Were they going to be kicked out of our chapter?

All of this was major just for a walk of trust that had ended up not putting us closer together but possibly tearing our line and chapter apart forever. It hadn't even been worth it!

Everyone was packing up their bags to head out as our adviser had asked. Reality was sinking in that we'd messed up. It broke my heart to see Isha and Sam crying. Even Cheryl was broken. She was standing near me saying repeatedly, "What have we done? What have we done? What have we done?"

Then some of us started bickering back and forth as to whether Dr. Garnes would actually follow through and turn us in. In reality, we had committed a cardinal crime. Each of us had signed a no-hazing policy, and all thirty-seven of us had stood in line blindfolded, caught red-handed like thieves in the night.

All I could do was pray. *Lord, just before Dr. Garnes came, I asked You to help us. Is this my fault? I wasn't sure whether someone was getting whooped up on. I needed you to free us from the terror, and maybe because of my prayer I summoned our adviser to intervene.*

I grabbed my head and just shook it. I had stopped praying at that moment. How could I be mad at God and question how He had answered my prayer? What was I, stupid? I was bringing even more tension and anguish into my life. I'd heard the saying "Be careful what you wish for because you just might get it many times before." But this was one of the first times I'd ever prayed, gotten my wish, and wanted to take back my words.

As I was the last one left in the room, I dropped to my knees and said, "Okay, Lord, forgive me. I'm just so new with this whole Christianity thing, and I don't know how to talk to You. I don't know what to specifically ask for. But You got to know I didn't want us to get in trouble when I asked You for help. So now that this is how You solved my problem, can You help me solve another one?

Can You make Dr. Garnes not say anything? Can You help her keep her mouth closed? Can You get her to understand they never touched us, and we were just in a line?"

Then I remembered a passage in the Book of Job: *The Lord gave, and the Lord taketh away; blessed be the name of the Lord.* Maybe this wasn't about my prayer or want I wanted. Maybe He didn't want Beta Gamma Pi for my life. So many people often said, "If you're a believer and a Christian, how can you be in a sorority?" That had never really phased me because Christianity had never been something that meant anything to my life, but now that it did, I wanted to live a life that would bring honor and glory to a majestic Lord and Savior. I was being a part of an organization founded on Christian principles.

Many in the organization particularly believed Christianity had used more venom, more nastiness than truth and love. If God didn't want me caught up in all that, would I be okay with His decision? That's what I felt something inside me was asking. I guess it had always been there, but again it was all new to me. I didn't know why I was wrestling with myself. I was now at a crossroads. Would I trust God with whatever He gave me, or would I continue to be caught up in needing to have it my way? Then it became crystal clear that I was getting a message from some internal force. *Go talk to Dr. Garnes yourself. Share with her your heart. See what happens.*

Sam ran back in the room. "Cassidy, we're waiting on you, girl. And we need you. Everyone is tripping. We feel we're messed up either way."

"Well, don't let them stress too much. Just stay in the

car. I need to go check on something real quick," I said, dashing around my girl.

"Where are you going?" Sam asked.

I didn't want to tell her, because I didn't know how the conversation with Dr. Garnes would go. I surely didn't want anybody putting all her hope on me.

I knocked on Dr. Garnes's hotel door. As soon as I knocked, I walked away, too nervous. I didn't get too far, though, because she answered.

"Cassidy, you okay? Your whole face is stressed. You having a relapse or something? You need to talk?"

"No, doc. I just came, on behalf of my line, to ask you to please give us another chance. We can't blame anyone but ourselves. We all want to be a part of Beta Gamma Pi so badly. Whatever we were asked to do, we would do. I know we've lost three girls on our line because they were participating in hazing. One could consider that we did the same thing. But we want to be here for Alpha chapter. We want to become Betas to change the system. We want to stand by the motto and make this world a better place. We want to please God as a chapter. We just ask for your compassion not to turn us in."

She looked over at me, surprised, and said, "I understand why you guys were doing that. My line was also taken over by some alumnae sorors years back, and when we crossed, a lot of colleges in Arkansas didn't want to have anything to do with us and considered us paper—not real or whatever. It was the most hurtful feeling. It took a long time for them to come around and understand we were hardworking Betas, as you said, ready to make our world better. I wouldn't wish that inadequate, isolated feeling on anybody. But the thing is, Cassidy, I now understand that people who feel that you need to be hazed in order to be worthy enough to join the sorority are the ones with the problem. We can't cater to wrong-doers. So tell your line sisters you get no more warnings. I know you were under dire pressure. Follow the rules from here on out, and y'all should be fine."

I sprung into her arms and hugged her tight. God had used me in a mighty way. Four days later, we stood in front of a limited number of Alpha chapter sorors be-cause some were suspended. Not all of them could wit-ness our meaningful initiation vow. I could not believe we had crossed. It felt wonderful, and I was so thankful that God had Beta Gamma Pi in the cards for me after all. I was not planning to let him down with what He'd entrusted me with.

It was the first sorority meeting. Thirty-seven excited new Betas stood ready to go through the formal opening ceremony that took place before every meeting, ready to go through the chapter's agenda, and ready just to be a part of the fold without feeling inferior. Our actual crossing-over ceremony hadn't been that special, but none of us cared. We hadn't had a decorated space and many gifts after we crossed, because the chapter was missing mem-bers due to the trust-walk incident that Dr. Garnes *did* report.

Torian, Loni, and the other Betas who had been with us that night on the walk of trust weren't allowed to par-ticipate with us as Pis. So that left Malloy and Alyx to work with the alumni sorors and bring us into the fold.

Though we had a ceremonial table, we were told later that we didn't get the nice facility, all the extra candles, and the well-decorated tables because frustration had set in that the line had been tampered with.

Though we weren't penalized, Alpha chapter was divided. Torian and her crew felt we weren't loyal to their cause and we needed to figure out a way to fix things with them. Personally, the threat didn't bother me, and now that I had my letters, I wasn't bending over backward to please them. The majority of my line felt differently though.

Malloy and Alyx had told us they were mad at their sisters, who were now my sisters. And somehow all of us had to find a way to not just coexist but act as one.

The actual opening ceremony was powerful and meaningful. We went through a vow and gave a reaffirmation statement saying we were committed to Beta Gamma Pi for life, and then we were able to start the chapter business. At the beginning there were no major issues.

Malloy was conducting the meeting as the President. We went through her report, the First Vice President's report, and the treasurer's report, and that's when we knew we were going to need to have some kind of fund-raiser because the funds were low. Even though they'd taken thirty-seven new members, a lot of the money they'd collected had had to go to the national organization. Next, we split into committees, and it was neat to see where I wanted to serve. Lots of sorors on my line started raising their hands, ready to volunteer. I was happy to know we were ready for business.

Dr. Garnes had to be excused for a second when she

was paged from work, and as soon as she left, Torian stood to her feet, got very indignant, and shouted, "I want her out. Dr. Garnes needs to be voted down as our adviser."

Loni stood next to her and said, "I know we're out of order, but we don't have much time before she brings herself back up in here. I want her out, too."

"Okay, well, because you know you're out of order," Malloy said, hitting the wooden gavel in her hand, "sit down."

The room burst with conversation. Everyone had to voice their opinion at that time. It was mayhem. Malloy banged the gavel louder.

Torian walked to the front of the room and snatched the object out of Malloy's hand. "Malloy, you might have the power, but this is our entire chapter. We talked to some of the new sorors, and they're behind us on this. We get to choose who our adviser is. Dr. Garnes is too uppity and old-fashioned to really be able to relate to all we have going on."

I couldn't believe what I was hearing. Dr. Garnes had basically saved my life, helped turn me around, and kept our line intact. How could Torian want to oust her? Even more incomprehensible, how could my line sisters want her to go?

Malloy stood and held out her hand for the gavel. Torian looked like she wasn't gonna give it back. Alyx got up and eyed Torian hard. Finally, Torian handed it back to Malloy.

Torian vented, "Handle it then."

Malloy hit the gavel again to settle us down, and once

we were quiet, she said, "We can't discuss this now. There is no formal motion on the floor."

Loni stood to her feet and said, "Fine, then I move that we ask Dr. Garnes to step down as our adviser."

"I second that motion," Torian said with her neck and eyes moving all crazy.

I had a lump in my throat. I felt sick all over. Why was this happening?

Malloy then said, "Is there any discussion?"

Quickly, I raised my hand. So did a lot of other people, but I wasn't called on. I was about to explode.

Malloy said, "The chair recognizes Isha."

Sensing she was outnumbered, Isha shyly said, "Don't you guys forget that she was the one who allowed our line to continue."

"Yeah!" Torian said sarcastically. "She did her job with the pledges. Now that we have a bigger chapter, we need a more progressive-thinking adviser, not a narrow-minded one. She's got to go!"

The parliamentarian at the back of the room, who'd been nonexistent up until that point, turned the lights off and on, and more noise erupted. "Madam President, I call for the question."

I wasn't up on parliamentarian procedures, but I knew that meant no one else was to talk and that it was time to take a vote. There were thirty-seven of us and eleven of them, so that meant forty-eight of us in the room. When the vote was cast, forty of them wanted her out. My heart sank. Sam was sitting beside me. She held my hand. She knew Dr. Garnes loved us and cared for us in ways that would be hard to replace.

When Dr. Garnes came back in the room, Malloy gave her the bad news. I didn't know how she was going to react—she'd served, and these chicks were ungrateful. But like the classy lady she was, she held her head high and didn't break down.

With a bit of emotion in her voice, she said, "It's been great serving you guys, and I understand if we're not a good match, that's fine. I've enjoyed my time with you. I pray that you all find the leader you want. I think all of you, and I do mean *all* of you, are great."

PISSED

As Dr. Garnes walked out of our chapter meeting room, steam was shooting out of my ears. I was so angry and disappointed in my sisters, knowing that they would kick Dr. Garnes to the curb. Our overwhelming majority vote quickly made me question if I even wanted to be a part of such thoughtlessness. What were they saying? If things didn't go their way, if they didn't like what was happening—even if what was happening was right— they would fight it? Just remove the situation from memory and not deal with the truth?

Torian and Loni and some of those other Betas had been wrong in coming to haze us. Though no one had been physically harmed, they had violated the no-hazing policy. And Dr. Garnes really could have had them suspended for good, yet she'd given them a pass and just told them to stay away from us until we crossed. I could have kicked myself for not seeing that there was something up. I mean, though we were a tight line, the last few days had been tough, and as I thought back further, I knew my sisters had been trying to figure out a way to get back into all of the Big Sisters' good graces. Instead of distancing myself from the drama, I should have stayed close to it to let them know they didn't need to cave like that.

With a little more arguing going on in the line, people were becoming antsy, not really believing we were going to cross and thinking Dr. Garnes would change her mind and expose us all. Because she hadn't, you would have thought they would have been loyal to her. Yet Torian had gotten to them, and the first chance they'd got at the first official meeting, they had cast the first vote, and she was out of there. After the vote, they had kept on going with the meeting as if nothing bad had happened; they hadn't even realized they were out of order because they technically couldn't conduct a meeting without an adviser present.

However, I couldn't just keep going on as if nothing had happened. You would have thought they were celebrating someone's birthday, but to me this was more like someone's funeral. I got so worked up I kicked my chair.

Sam tugged at my arm. "We got outvoted. We tried. There is nothing else we can do, Cass. We're supposed to go along with the majority."

I knew that's what we had learned when we were pledging, that you might not always win a chapter vote but you were supposed to support the chapter's decision.

But to me, that was as severe as if the chapter had voted to rob a bank—because we said we'd do it, would I go along with something criminal? I tugged my arm away from my girl and dashed out the door.

Frantically searching and then finding our ex-adviser, I said, "Dr. Garnes, wait up, please! I want to talk to you. I'm so sorry this happened. Those girls are jerks."

"Cassidy, I'm fine, sweetheart. However, you need to go tell your sisters they can't have a meeting without an adviser present. But something tells me at this point they don't care. I do want you to keep doing what's right, though. You don't have to worry about you being seen with me."

"I'm fine." This wasn't right, and I was not going for it. Something had to be done.

A plan came to mind. "You should fight this. We should fight this. They can't just get rid of you without going through the Regional Coordinator, right? Plus, they can't oust the adviser right in the middle of the semester."

"Wow, I'm surprised you've been reading the chapter manual handbook. They're not able to, but sometimes you know when you're tired and you know when you don't even want to prolong something that's not working. I came onto this position because I care about this chapter and you young ladies. I do have high standards for our sorority, as we all should, but I'm not gonna let collegiates take the short road. I am also not going to stay and try to input my wisdom into knucklehead, hard-headed, fast-behind girls. Sometimes you have to lose something before you really appreciate how good you had it, and sometimes you're not the only one who can make a difference. And I'm begining to realize, the chapter and I may need to part from each other, Cassidy."

Wow! Dr. Garnes really wanted what was best for Alpha chapter and not what felt good for herself. To me it seemed humiliating, and yet she didn't take it that way at all. She was saying she wished us all well and she'd be praying for us. We talked a few more moments about my disappointment.

"I just want to make sure you're okay," Dr. Garnes said. "You have a lot you're dealing with and not dealing with, and though I am not going to be your adviser, you know you always have an open door to talk to me any time you need."

She gave me a big hug. I didn't want this to end. I wanted her to see my side and get ready to fight my bull-headed chapter sorors. I knew what was best for our chapter—she was. Unfortunately, she wanted to let it go; the chapter sorors had let *her* go. I neither agreed with, nor could do anything about, either decision. As she walked away to her car, I knew we had let a good one slip away, and I was angry.

It was finally Christmastime. And as hard as the semester had been, I had managed pledging, a tough schedule, and all the emotional ups and downs. However, I was so happy to get a break and go home. I still hated a lot about my upbringing. I hated that I was from a poor family, I hated that Christmas had always been modest when I was growing up, and I hated that though we didn't have much, my mom allowed her sister and brother to mooch off us.

My aunt Sally was five years older than me and had never had a job—had never even finished high school—and my mom thought it was okay to allow her to find her way on our time. She'd help Sally get new clothes and other stuff, and it bothered me because it actually took away from my own food and clothes. My mom felt like she had to be Sally's mom because their mother had died when Sally was two. My uncle Bill had done well in high school sports. He'd had colleges scouting him from all over the southeast for baseball. However, his grades had been so horrible he couldn't pass the graduation test to sustain any offer. When he'd become a senior and didn't graduate and watched his dreams go by the wayside, he'd turned angry.

My last few years of high school, Bill had been playing ball in some minor league. He should have been sending money back to my mom, but she'd said he was blowing it on alcohol and drugs. Now that no one wanted him to play anymore, due to a busted knee, he was back at her house doing nothing.

When I walked into my mom's house, I could have thrown up. The whole place smelled like smoke. When my mom asked me if I wanted to go with her to the grocery store, I jumped at the chance. You would have thought they would have had the place clean and stocked with groceries for my homecoming. Not!

As soon as we were in the car alone together, I said, "Mom, I don't understand why you put up with the two of them wasting their lives away and milking you for all you've got. Those are grown folks living off their big sister. They are not kids anymore. Kick them out, shoot."

"You don't understand, Cassidy. We've had it hard. Family sticks together. That's the one thing I remember my mom instilling in me so much. When you graduate from college and get that good job, I'm going to hope you'll . . ."

Okay, I couldn't even listen to anything else she was saying at that point. I rolled my eyes and became tense at the idea that I would become my family's breadwinner. I was supposed to go to college and then help take care of all three of them? She was really tripping, worse than a person locked in the crazy house.

"Why are you rolling your eyes?" she said as we got to the grocery store and walked inside, grabbing a cart. "I hope you haven't lost your mind thinking you better than people and stuff. I meant what I said. You supposed to help us."

"No, Mom, I don't think I'm better than anybody. I just work hard for what I have. I don't mind helping people who help themselves, but I'm not going to do all the work and then sit there and let somebody betray me by not even trying in their own life. I mean, that's just crazy. They are scheming you."

"Watch your mouth. Watch how you talk to me. I've given the three of you the shirt off my back. I don't deserve no sass talk."

"That's fine, Mom. I apologize. I know they're your brother and sister and you love your family," I said.

Then I explained that I actually hated that I had even come home because I didn't want to have a confrontation with her. It seemed she wasn't trying to listen to anything I had to say, so I just stopped trying. We were at the same impasse we'd been for most of my life.

When we got back to her place, I could not believe her sister was going through my stuff and actually had on one of my outfits. We were family, so what was the issue, right? Well, how about she was a size twenty, and I was a size eight!

Yanking my dress out of her hands before she could pull it apart to get in it, I said, "I can't believe you got your hands in all my stuff! Why are you wearing my clothes? You ain't even ask nobody. You're stretching it! You're going to pay me back for this."

"Chill out," she said, pushing me back against the wall and taking the purple silk outfit from me.

"Don't tell me to chill out!" I lunged toward her to try to grab my garment back.

The next thing I knew, my uncle was grabbing my waist and pulling me to him, whispering, "Aw, Cassidy, you know you need to calm down and chill out. We're family. We share everything. Relax."

When he said that and wouldn't let me go, it struck a cord that pierced my soul. His yucky hands were sliding around on me, and that gesture was too eerie and familiar. I felt helpless, like a child needing someone to rescue me from harm, but no one would. What was this about?

Oh, my gosh. The past I'd blocked out suddenly dawned on me as his voice kept talking in my ear. I could see his body on top of me. I could hear that same voice telling me to relax and calm down and enjoy it. He was the one who had violated me so young.

I just started pounding on his chest and screaming, "I hate you! You raped me! I was little. How could you do that!"

He immediately let me go. He didn't move, and I didn't either. This was more than I needed to remember.

Shaking, Sally came over to us and said, "What? What are you talking about?"

"I can't believe this! I have been thinking all this time that I was crazy. The nightmares—I couldn't put them together. I couldn't understand. I guess I blocked them out because the uncle who should have protected me like a brother took advantage of me."

I kicked him and hit him and punched him in his chest, and he didn't fight back. He didn't deny it. He didn't tell me to calm down or say, "Cassidy, no, it wasn't me." He just dropped to the floor.

"What in the world is going on in here?" my mom screamed.

Tears were streaming down my face. Everything I had been going through—so promiscuous, always thinking sex was the answer, needing to feel loved—stemmed from him taking advantage of me as a child. I wanted him to pay. I wanted him to burn. I wanted him to feel as horrible as I had felt for years. I certainly wasn't going to protect him for my mom, who thought he was perfect.

I shouted at the top of my lungs, *"Your precious brother raped me years ago!"*

"No," my mom said as she backed out of my room.

"No, no. Bill would never do that. He had girls coming out of the woodwork. I had to keep them off him. He would never ruin my child, his niece. Tell her, Bill. Tell her!"

Sally rushed over to me, looked me in the eye, and saw that there was no way I could be lying. She went to her brother and slapped him hard. "Was misusing me not enough?"

My mom screamed out, "What?"

I wiped my tears and thought, *What?* Had Sally been through my same tormented ordeal? Did she now have an excuse for never amounting to much—because her own brother had taken her innocence? Bill needed to be behind bars somewhere.

"Yeah, why you think I'm so messed up?" Sally said as she went over to her sister. "Life has been hard because my brother misused me. I never knew he was doing the same to your little girl."

"How could you, Bill?" my mom said sadly, clearly letting us know this was the worst news of her life. "I can't believe you'd do this to me. I've given you everything I had. I took you in. I cared for you when no one else would, and you do this to my daughter? You misused my trust? Get out of here!"

She yelled more cuss words than I knew existed as she charged up to him, but he didn't move. She ran to the kitchen and grabbed a knife. It took everything Sally and I had to hold her back. But, fighting us off, she got loose and went for him.

BLAME

Seeing my mother with a sharp butcher knife in her hand scared me. I had never seen her eyes fire red before. Her temples were bulging outta her head. And though her body was trembling, the knife was held right at my uncle's throat.

"I loved you. I would've given my life for yours. But right now I'm gonna take yours instead. You don't deserve to live. How could you, Bill?"

"Mom!" I screamed. "No! He's not worth it, Mom. Please drop it. He's not important enough." I stepped in at that moment and grabbed the blunt, steel object and took it away from my mother.

She fell into my arms, saying, "I can't believe I didn't know."

"I hate you!" Sally screamed, kicking Uncle Bill while

he was down on the floor. He was too frightened to move one muscle.

"Mom, are you okay?"

"You got all this damage that can't be erased, and you're worried about me?" She pulled back.

"Sis," Bill said, approaching my mom and grabbing her leg, "I'm sorry."

She snarled, "There's nothing you can say to ease this situation. Get the heck outta my house now before I change my mind and end it all for you. Bill, you done made me crazy! I hate you. Leave."

"Where am I supposed to go? I ain't got nothing or nowhere to be," he said with tears in his eyes.

"All those women you bring over my house—go stay with one of them. Go live on the streets and become humble so you can understand the innocence you stole from my child and your sister. Looking at you turns my stomach. You're a nasty bastard."

My mom picked up the lamp from the family room, yanked the plug from the wall, and threw it at the back of his head. It shattered while he ran out of the house without looking back.

I just sank on the couch, rocking back and forth, re-playing over and over again in my mind what I now remembered. Everything he'd done to me was so disgusting. Once the memories came flooding back like a dam that had been broken, I knew every horrifying detail.

I was finally confronting my past and what had happened to me. As I sat there weeping, I finally understood that what had happened to me was not my fault.

* * *

The next few days, when my mom was at work and my aunt was off doing her own thing, my uncle would come around begging me for food, begging me to let him take a bath but, most irritatingly, begging me to forgive him.

Uncle Bill pleaded, "Cassidy, I know I was wrong. I've thought about it a lot, and I didn't mean to hurt you like that. I thought you would let it fly, or that maybe it didn't even happen—"

"It didn't even happen?" I said, completely cutting him off. "Night after night, I can't even breathe, let alone sleep. I keep going over it again and again in my head. Why did I want to be so promiscuous? Because you exposed me to something too early and in absolutely the wrong way. It did so much damage I allowed myself to be violated again just a few months ago. I've been on medication just to clear my head of the incident, so forgiving you is definitely out of the question!"

He stood there, tripping on my honesty. He looked away, so sad. I shoved a piece of fried chicken and bread in his hand and slammed the door in his face.

My mom wanted me to stay through New Year's, but there was just no way. Over the holiday my house became the most unbearable place. My sorority sisters wanted me to party with them, but I wasn't down for their excitement either. My family was irreconcilably damaged, and that was nothing to celebrate.

And I guess Isha knew I didn't wanna be alone because she suggested I go with her to watch night service. Truth be told, seeing Konner Black again didn't sound too bad.

He intrigued me. I wasn't sure if the idea of being in his presence or allowing the Spirit to make me whole again was pushing me more to want to join Isha.

Either way, I got dressed and was ready to leave at ten PM. We arrived at the packed church a few minutes after the service had started. Quickly, we sat in the pews, joining other high school and college kids to hear Konner Black preach.

"You think you can start the New Year off doing the same shady things you did this year? You're wrong. God wants to change your heart in the New Year and leave your past in the old one. But let me keep it real. You might have to forgive some people to truly move on to the high calling and the place God wants you to be."

Okay, now I was squirming in my seat. I didn't need to hear him speak about forgiveness. Yeah, it was cool for God to forgive me, but for me to forgive somebody else . . . particularly my uncle? Was this a joke? Was I being punked in the sanctuary? I wanted to scream, but Konner wouldn't let up. He kept preaching about how God wanted us to forgive, to go to our brother and fix things, and if we could ask God to forgive us our sins, how could we expect that to happen when we couldn't pardon anyone else? If we loved God and allowed Him to live in our hearts, we couldn't have hearts that were hard. We had to be loving, generous, and kind—give people the benefit of the doubt, in hopes that they would find God to change them from their wicked ways, accept forgiveness, and become better.

I was so inspired by the end of the message I was practically in tears. I had been so selfish, I'd just left a note telling my mom I was going back to school. I knew my mom would have stopped me, and I didn't want that, so I'd done things my way, not caring if I hurt her.

From one of the payphones in the church I called home. My mom picked up and said, "I didn't even get a chance to say good-bye to you. I'm so sorry."

"I know, Mom, I'm sorry, too. I just had to get outta there."

"I got your note, and I apologize that you were experiencing so much pain here."

"It's okay now. God's got my back, Mom. He's got us all."

"I wanna tell her I'm sorry again," I heard Uncle Bill saying in the background.

"She doesn't wanna speak to you. You're only here to eat and then leave. Nothing else."

"Mom, can I talk to him, please?" I heard them arguing, but she handed him the phone. Before he could say anything, I said, "Uncle Bill, you stole something precious from me, and I've been damaged because of it. But . . . I forgive you."

There were no strings attached. There were no preconditions. There was nothing God needed to do for me in the New Year. I just needed to move on, forgive, and obey God's Word and hope that the one who'd wronged me would find God. After all, Konner had said we all fell short to the glory of God, and we all needed another chance to get right again.

"I was hoping you didn't leave," the fine reverend said, startling me before I was able to head back into the sanctuary.

"No, I just had to make a phone call," I said in a giddy voice, intrigued that he was looking for me.

"Did you maybe wanna go get something to eat?" he asked after a long, awkward pause.

"Being that it's New Year's, don't you think everywhere will be crowded?" I couldn't think of anything else to say.

"I just wanna spend some time getting to know you, that's all." He reached out and grabbed my hand, placing his other hand on my cheek and stroking it gently. "You're a beautiful girl. I look out when I'm preaching a lot and notice you're really into my sermons. Sometimes on your face I can tell you've had pain and issues you've gone through that were not good at all. Maybe I can be a part of your life now and give you good memories from this point on. You deserve only the best."

Okay. He'd had me when he'd told me he'd hoped I hadn't left. Now he was stroking my cheek and making me feel extra special. "Uh, I came here with Isha."

"Well, I don't think that's gonna be a big problem."

"What do you mean?" I asked.

"She likes Mark, the music director. I think the two of them are planning to hang out." *I can't believe my girl didn't tell me,* I thought. But I was happy for her. He continued, "She just wanted me to catch up with you and let you know she'd be downstairs if I found you."

Processing what he said, I asked, "She thought I left, too? I didn't mean to scare anyone."

"Are you okay? Was my sermon so bad you had to leave? I know you said you had to make a phone call, and I don't mean to pry, but what's going on with you?"

I wanted to tell him about my crazy world and how I didn't want to let him in before we knew each other a little. But I didn't take that route. I didn't open up either. I liked the thought of taking things slow and smoothing out the road. "It's gonna be kinda different for me dating a minister."

"Why is that?" he asked, letting go of my hand and giving me a look that made me feel pure, beautiful, and lovely. "No one is perfect. But you can let a godly man take care of you and make this dating relationship perfect in His sight, by treating you like the queen you are. You down for that?"

I was speechless. So we went out that night and for the next seven days as well.

There was another week before school would start. Sam hadn't come back to our apartment yet. For our seventh date, I invited Konner over for dinner and dessert. I thought it was gonna be hard for me to be close to another guy after what I'd gone through with Al Dutch and my uncle. But spending time with Konner at the movies, at the bowling alley, in the library while I studied, and as he prepared his sermons—we just connected.

The whole week I learned so much about him. He hadn't gone to college but to a trade school instead. He'd been selling drugs and wanted to end his life until a youth pastor told him God was the only way to true happiness. From that point on, he had changed for the better.

We talked more over dinner at my place. He loved my meal; the Cornish hens with orange carrot wine sauce, asparagus, and baked potato warmed his belly. Afterward I served him a piece of my homemade cheesecake with cherries drizzled on top.

My emotions were getting out of control, and I had to figure out what to do with them. He was looking so good sitting across from me. Shucks, I wanted him for dessert. So I took my hand and started to feed him. He was smiling. I moved to the other side of the table and sat on his lap. He was moaning. The next bite I fed him, I touched my lips to his. Next thing you knew, we were hot and into each other.

Finally, he stood up and said, "I'm sorry if I misled you, Cassidy, but we can't go down this road. I'm supposed to lead us in this relationship, so we'll do it right. Though you're so attractive and you've done nothing wrong, I don't want you to think I wanna be with you because of your body. I want to be with you because I want your heart. And if I made you think otherwise, I'm the one to blame."

11

GRILL

"Please, it's fine. Just get out of my face," I finally said out of frustration when Konner kept trying to rationalize ending our moment of passion.

He just kept going on and on, trying to make me feel like it was okay that I'd been really aggressive. But it wasn't okay. It wasn't okay for our relationship, and it wasn't okay for me, now that I knew why I was like that. There was still a part deep inside of me that couldn't change; all I knew was how to make a guy physically aroused. If I had any more to offer that would keep a man intrigued, I had absolutely no clue what that was, and I was too embarrassed, ashamed, and upset to try to figure it out at that moment.

"Cassidy, please, settle down. Let's be open about what happened. I really don't what to leave right now," he said in a soft, understanding tone. "I really want to talk you through this."

But I wasn't listening to what he was saying. I just saw his mouth yapping, and because I was already annoyed, I opened the front door and gestured for him to get out. If he never came back, I knew I'd regret it, but for now, because I was an impulse girl, Konner Black had to jet.

"I'd like to pray before I leave, if I could," he said, reaching for my hand before I tugged it back.

I didn't want to laugh in his face or tell him what a dumb idea I thought that was, so I just shook my head, opened the door even wider, and sort of shoved him out of it.

"Thanks, but no thanks," I finally said.

"Well, I'll be praying for you, and there's nothing you can do about that," he said as he walked out.

At that moment, when I shut the door, I started slowly releasing tears. He was a good man, and I had just kicked him out of my place. I certainly regretted the fact that part of me had told him to go. I jumped in a hot shower, hoping to soak away the anguish I felt, but I just kept hearing, *You're never going to get a good man. You wouldn't know how to treat him if you had one. You're so pathetic, throwing yourself on a minister. What you doing, trying to make him fall? Girl, you tried to ruin a man of the cloth. You deserve to be alone.*

Under the hot, steamy water, I just screamed until I cried. I cried until I was out of breath. Then I prayed. *Lord, help me. Forgive me. Help me be like You. Help me.*

I woke up the next morning feeling renewed, like it was

going to be a great day. A part of me wanted to call Konner and apologize, but I knew we both needed space. The dance team was going to perform at some of the basketball games, and we had to practice our routine for the national dance competition. My team had had a couple practices during Christmas break, but because I'd gone home, I wasn't there. The band director knew this, but I could tell there was tons of tension when I got to practice.

"Um, did somebody move the time up or something?" I said. They were all in the middle of a dance number.

"Tried to leave you a message," Ginger said, "but your voice mail was full. We just felt we needed some extra work to get ready. But you know this routine. You can fall in and get it."

And then Meagan, who had recently been dressing even sluttier than I ever could, walked up to my face and said, "Why don't you just quit this squad? You're half here, and when you *are* here, we're supposed to just make exceptions for you, bend the rules and stuff? Everybody's tired of that. Everybody's tired of you."

Ginger stepped between us and said, "All right, get back, Meagan. Director Saxton knew where she was."

"Don't either one of y'all touch me," Meagan said out of nowhere. Ginger and I looked at her like she was crazy because no one was touching her paranoid behind.

"If you don't get out of my face I'm going to do more than touch you," I told her. She started shoving me, and I started shoving her back. I don't know what her problem was, but I wasn't a punk.

Meagan yelled out, "Both of y'all are just jealous that I'm Al Dutch's girl now!"

The anger on my face turned to pity. I looked at Ginger, and she looked back at me. The two of us had never talked about our relationships with Al Dutch, but I got the feeling it hadn't been all good for her, and I had pretty much told her I thought he was crazy. But yet here was another girl standing before us defending his honor.

So I walked away, saying, "I'm not quitting the team. I'm here to practice. You can have Al Dutch."

"Oh, girl, please. I already do," she said, working her neck. "I didn't need your permission for that. You better not call him over to your place again."

Obviously, he had used me to tell her some lie. I was so through with her I didn't even care to clear my name. The loudmouth know-it-all could think whatever she wanted. She had just better not come charging at me again.

"Okay, Cassidy, just because we got rid of the adviser doesn't mean you can't be a part of the chapter anymore," Samantha said to me later that night when we were chilling back at our place.

"I just feel like if you don't stand for something, Sam, you'll fall for anything, and it wasn't right for them to get rid of her. I know you didn't vote for it, and I'm not mad at anybody for doing what they did, but that doesn't mean I have to jump up and down and be excited to be a Beta when they're doing stupid stuff. And this party you all are having tonight, what's the point?"

"The point is for us to raise some money so we can do more community service projects. If you'd come to the meetings . . ." She paused.

"Please, girl. The meetings you are having illegally because you don't have an adviser there to mediate, you mean?"

"See, now you're talking technicality stuff. What are we supposed to do, just kill time and wait till we get a new one?"

I lashed out. "It was y'all's decision to think irrationally to get rid of the lady. Yeah, you're supposed to wait. Our chapter is still on probation, both from the school and from Grand Chapter, so all of us have a responsibility, Sam, to make sure that we follow the letter of the law all the way around so we don't do anything to jeopardize this chapter. But the Betas are just planning some campus party and having meetings without an adviser present. Y'all are just thinking you can make your own rules, and I'm not down with that."

"Well, everybody wants you to be there. Even Torian and Loni," Sam said in a sweet voice.

"Yeah, right, they haven't called me and asked me anything." I wasn't tricked by her kindness.

She slid down near me and said, "They thought I would have a better shot at getting you to come."

"Why would they want me there?" I said.

"Because you see a different side," Sam explained. "You can be there to make sure nothing goes wrong. If nothing else, you love the chapter. You being there will keep everybody on their toes. You said they think haphazardly, so be there. We can get this right. Please."

I don't know how she talked me into it, but a couple of hours later I was walking around the old gymnasium in which we were hosting our new-semester jam. I had to admit the deejay they had hired was off the chain. He had the latest beats, and from the get-go, even with the small crowd, any time somebody came in the door, they headed right to the dance floor to groove.

"Thanks for coming." Torian came up behind me.

"I don't think what you did to Dr. Garnes was right," I told her right off the bat so she didn't misunderstand that she and I still had big issues.

"I understand," she said, "but we're sisters. We're not going to agree on everything, but we're always family. Come on, Cass, let's party. You know I know you can throw down. Give me some love."

Though we hugged, I was still apprehensive. I mean, Torian couldn't even comprehend the fact that she was completely wrong, and if family broke the law, they still needed to be reprimanded for it. Yet she thought she was above all that. So though we had to exist in the same sorority, I knew we weren't going to be best buddies. Besides, she hadn't liked me from the beginning because she'd thought I was wild, and I would never forget how mean she'd treated me.

All of a sudden I got shoved hard in the back. The push was so abrupt it moved my body five feet forward.

When I turned back, Torian defended me and said, "Hey, hey, what's going on? What are you doing? You need to leave with all that."

My mouth hung open; Meagan was standing there. Her hands were motioning for more. I walked back to her, and she shoved me again.

"You need to stay out of this," Meagan said to Torian as Torian looked about to slug her. "This is between me and your slimy sorority sister who can't keep her hands off my man. Messing up my perfect world."

"What are you talking about?" I said, knowing Al Dutch had fed her more bologna to cover his own lies.

"Al told me you've been calling him and texting him and you won't leave him alone. He was over at your place today to end it, and you put a hickey on his neck. Then he found out that—"

"I don't know what he's been telling you or why he's been making you think I want to be with him. You're the one who needs an eye-opener. He's a jerk, and I don't care if I ever see him again. Don't believe the hype. I despise Al Dutch."

"You're just saying that," she said as she shoved me again. "Of course you'd try to leave him now."

I'd had enough. She was making my blood boil. I pushed her to the ground.

As soon as I raised my hand to hit her in the mouth, Torian stopped me. "It ain't worth it, girl, for real."

I huffed. The party had ceased, and all eyes were on us.

"You need to get on out of here," Torian said and stepped in Meagan's way.

"Get on. We don't want any trouble at our party," I told Meagan. "You need to talk to Al Dutch and get him to tell you the truth. He was not with me."

"This ain't over. Y'all Betas make me sick thinking you can have whatever you want because you wear some Greek letters. Y'all need to stop spreading stuff. I paid my money, and I ain't going nowhere," Meagan said as she and a few of the other girls from the dance team followed her.

I stood face to face with Torian, not knowing what to say. I guess I owed her a thank you, but it just wouldn't come out. The whole night was crazy.

"We protect family. Don't let her get to you," Torian said to me.

I nodded and just went my own way, furious. It was too late. I was so upset. I knew if anyone said anything too off the wall, we'd both go up in smoke.

I was walking around the party silently, and everybody was having fun. Because of the incident with Meagan, the excitement and vibe I was feeling for the jam had quickly subsided. The girl had to go psycho, fronting on me with some bull Al Dutch had told her. The gall of him. If I did ever cross paths with him again, he'd better not even front like we're cool.

Alyx came over to me and said, "It's hard being in a sorority, huh? But you wanted it. I'm sure you didn't think it'd be this messy, but I'm glad to see you here."

I didn't know how to respond to her, because it was hard and I did want it and I didn't know if I was happy to be in the place. I'd much rather be at home. But even if I was there, I'd be thinking of my sorors and hoping they would not be getting themselves into trouble. Yet here I was about to hit someone.

"You and Torian will work through your differences. I'm a little salty with her, too, for letting Dr. Garnes go, but I just saw what she did," Alyx said.

"Yeah, she had my back, and so?" I said, acting as if I didn't care.

"And so I know that mattered to you. I know that meant something. We're about to stroll. This is your first time as a Beta. Now, the Cassidy I know loves to show her stuff, and I think I'm the queen of it, too, so you just need to come on with me and let's get that smirk off your face." I didn't budge. "Seriously, everybody has their own way of showing that they care about each other. We are dysfunctional, but we are Alpha chapter. Enjoy this with us."

"But you're okay with the fact that there's no adviser here? That we could get in so much trouble if we're caught? People can start something with us or turn us in. There is so much wrong here," I said, hoping the girl I admired felt the severity of what was happening.

"Nothing is going to happen. We won't get caught. I'm not okay with it, but the chapter voted on it. So Malloy, as the President, and me, as VP, have to go along. That's just one of our rules—when the vote doesn't go your way, you don't walk away. You know?"

I nodded.

The deejay got the word from Malloy, who had called the sorors to hit the floor. Alyx smiled my way and gestured for me to follow her. Maybe a good jam would help me ease up. To the dance floor I went.

My sorors chanted the moves they made. "Stepping to the left and stepping to the right, stepping up, stepping back and side to side. We are swinging our hips from the left to the right. Beta women are out of sight."

And I fell in line naturally, ready to repeat the pattern. We were grooving, and all girls with other letters and no letters wanted ours. Yes, BGP was more than about partying, but throwing down was surely one of the perks to membership. It was a privilege to represent.

"Y'all know the rules. So don't be no fool!" Torian yelled out as she called the next chant. "Nobody cuts the line, this is Beta time! Get back, everybody, here we come, here we come! Get back, everybody, BGP is number one!"

The next part of her step was where we made the line tighter and dared anyone to break it. We weaved in and out of the crowd, and people were chanting and cheering for us.

Cheryl came from nowhere and started spinning round and round. Her eyes were red, and she looked like she hadn't combed her hair in days. She was mouthing the word *Al.* I wanted to scream out, "Girl, don't be looking for that nut Al Dutch. Be done with that." One of our sorors pulled her in line with her.

However, we couldn't keep the line moving. Meagan came over, broke up the line, and said to Cheryl, "I know you, of all people, don't have the nerve to look for my man. I done told y'all Betas—"

"I'm not in the mood, girl," Cheryl said.

"Don't let anybody cut the line! This is our pride line! Move it up there! Keep it tight, keep it tight!" Torian yelled from the back.

"I'm not here to dance," Cheryl said to us. "I need to find—"

Before she could say anything, Meagan shoved her like she had me earlier. She pulled Cheryl's hair. Sam pulled Meagan off Cheryl.

"She's crazy," I whispered in Cheryl's ear when I helped her off the floor.

"She need not mess with me now," Cheryl said, obviously dealing with something heavy.

"I'll show you crazy. What do I have to lose now, thanks to one of you malicious Betas. Come on, y'all!" Meagan said, motioning for some of the other dancers to break our line.

When they were successful, Cheryl went ballistic. She took the girl by the collar and threw her to the ground. This was getting out of hand.

Meagan kept screaming, "Leave me alone! Get off me! I already have to go to the doctor, thanks to you. Stop!"

And Cheryl kept saying, "No, you're big and bad! You think you all that! What you going to do?"

Then Cheryl punched Meagan with a left hook and then a right one. Cheryl hit her again until there was blood all in Meagan's grill.

POINTLESS

Everyone was telling Cheryl to get off Meagan, but our words went in one ear and out the other. With now more than forty Betas on the scene—and the fact that most of my line wore turquoise jackets decorated with our line name, 37 DEGREES BELOW, and the Greek letters BGP in purple—it could've been any of our sisters infusing the pain. Not one Beta could tell who was fighting.

Alyx walked over to Cheryl to stop her. I went over, too. The two of us tugged and tugged until we pulled Cheryl off Meagan. As soon as we were successful, about ten of us dashed to the ladies' bathroom.

Samantha guarded the door, and Alyx let her have it. "Are you crazy? What were you thinking, Cheryl?"

"I'm sorry. Torian shouted not to let anybody break the line, and I guess for a moment I just snapped. She kept pushing me, and I needed to find out if this was true, and she just pushed me the wrong way. This is a lot that has been dumped on me. I just . . . I don't know," Cheryl said in one breath, not making much sense to any of us.

"Find out if what is true, Cheryl? So, you would risk possibly losing your letters over some girl who got in your face? Grow up, Cheryl. We have to deal with bad news from time to time. That is no reason to try to kill someone."

Cheryl seemed still in a daze. Her eyes were roaming, and it was very apparent she still needed to find Al Dutch. She then started calling his name.

Of course at that point I really hated that I hadn't let them all know what Al Dutch had done to me because since I'd kept quiet, he'd been through many more women, victimizing them in so many ways. We were all so damaged. It just seemed like there was no way we could ever be repaired. Cheryl's typical actions weren't of the tough girl I was used to dealing with. Al had done something to her. I just knew it.

"You gotta get cleaned up!" Sam yelled. "One of the girls says someone called the police, and they are on their way."

"The police!" Alyx yelled. "Oh, my gosh. We're gonna lose our chapter."

Those of us who were in the bathroom got scared. Well, everyone but Cheryl. She was still wigged out. Everything I thought could go wrong had happened, and more. Bottom line: there was no excuse for us having a campus event without the presence of a collegiate adviser. But we had, something had gone wrong, and now the campus police were on their way to find us.

"Guys, we gotta clear all these people out of here,"

Alyx said. "If we go out there now with this blood still on Cheryl, they're gonna know a Beta did this."

"We stand as one," Loni said; I hadn't even realized she was in the room with us. She walked over to Cheryl and said, "You better hope this girl doesn't have to go to the hospital. We were telling you to get off her! Okay—so what if Torian told you to respect the line. You gotta know when to face reality and admit defeat. You lost either way. Are you happy? Stop looking so crazy. Cheryl? Cheryl?"

Cheryl did not respond, and I was so worried Al had done something to her. I knew that after my night with Al, I had been so vulnerable and beside myself. What if what we had seen from Cheryl was just the beginning? Someone needed to get her to a hospital before she did herself more harm.

"Come on outta there! Everybody come out now!" Malloy yelled from outside the door. "The cops are here."

Sam was trying to wipe the blood from Cheryl, who was so stiff and cold, it was as though she didn't even care if she got in trouble.

"I just can't let her take the fall for this, you guys. She didn't know what she was doing. She snapped, okay?" Sam said, crying. "Something is very wrong with her. Am I the only one who sees that?"

Sam wasn't the only one who knew Cheryl was tripping, so I grabbed another wet rag and helped get the blood off. This all just seemed so surreal. Was I helping someone get rid of the evidence of a crime, or was I being a good sister? What would God say was right? I was so confused. When we all walked outside, the police said an ambulance was on the way to get Meagan. She was unable to talk and unable to tell them who had brutally battered her face.

One stern, pale city officer looked ready to take us all in and asked us, "Who did this?"

The campus police behind him wanted one of us to speak up. One campus cop didn't look like he wanted the real police on the scene. Seemed the faster we spoke up and answered the real cop's questions, the quicker he'd be off Western Smith's property. However, none of us said a word.

"Any time the ambulance is called, the city police get dispatched in," the campus cop said to us, "so somebody better get your adviser to the scene quick. We've been looking all over for her. One person said she was in the bathroom. One person said she was in the parking lot waiting for the cops. Why do we keep getting the runaround here? I know you ladies aren't doing anything illegal, particularly when your chapter is on probation."

Everyone looked around, not knowing what to do. We had no adviser there. I walked over to a corner and called Dr. Garnes. I was sure she would understand that we needed her badly. She had to come up here and help us. Though they had kicked her out, they were now at her mercy. If only she would pick up the phone.

Finally, after a ton of rings, she answered. I was talking fast, so she asked me to slow down. I needed her to quickly understand what I had to say and hurry to the scene.

I was extremely dumbfounded when she said, "I'm sorry, Cassidy, but you girls are on a collision course, and this was bound to happen. How are y'all ever gonna learn if I keep covering up everything? I'm sorry. I am not your adviser. Good night, I'll pray for y'all."

She hung up the phone, and I wondered why I had even called her in the first place. That had been a waste of time. Walking back over to my sorors, I knew we were in big trouble.

Perturbed, I took my phone and threw it across the room. Sam caught it. She and Isha rushed over to me.

Sam handed me the phone and said, "Cass, what are you doing, girl? Don't you realize there are cops all around? Are you trying to hit somebody in the eye and get taken in for that?"

"I'm just frustrated, annoyed, and irritated right about now."

"We should've listened to you," Isha said. "We never should have thrown a party. We just got in the sorority, and now it's gone."

Isha was so emotional, Sam was so nervous, and I was so angry. There was not one thing any of us could do to stop what was going on around us. The police were interviewing everybody for criminal evidence. The campus police were taking everyone's statements to find information that could possibly kick us off campus.

"I just can't believe she would do us like that. I thought she really cared," I finally said to my two girls. "Coming up here to stand in as our adviser would not have killed her."

"What, you tried to call Dr. Garnes?" Isha asked.

Hitting my phone against my leg, I said, "Yeah, and she's not coming."

"Well, can you blame her?" Sam agreed.

"Yeah, I blame her. We need her badly, and she won't bail us out," I said.

"That's because we kicked her out," Sam said, rubbing my shoulders so I could calm down.

"Wait, I didn't want her gone. I was on her side. I'd been mad at everybody else because of it, and Dr. Garnes knew that."

"She probably thinks you're a fool to be with us," Isha said.

"I think I'm a fool to be with y'all, too, but Sam insisted I come," I said.

"To keep us out of trouble," Sam said.

Isha said, "Why couldn't one of you stop Cheryl from hitting that girl? Y'all were right beside each other in line."

"When has anybody been able to stop Cheryl? You should know that better than any of us," Sam said. "Plus, for real, she is acting different."

"She's right about that," Isha said as I finally looked down at my phone.

There were cracks all over the dial screen from my throw. Just what I deserved. I mean, absolutely nothing was going right. Certainly, I didn't expect to have a tantrum and not have consequences.

"So what are we going to tell the police when they come over here? What are we going to say? Are we going to say who did this, or are we supposed to stand and be silent? I'm asking because I wanna tell on Cheryl. Alpha chapter is more important than any individual, right?" Isha asked. "Cheryl is our girl and all, but, guys, we can't lose our chapter."

"You can't tell," Sam quickly responded. "You just said it—Cheryl is our girl, and she needs our silence. Where is she anyway?"

The two of them argued their points back and forth, and I was stuck. I could see both sides, and I could see no matter how much I tried to do the right thing, the wrong thing always happened, and people always disappointed me.

"Hey, can I talk to you for a minute?" a familiar yet unwanted voice said from behind me.

Sam and Isha stopped fussing. I should've known the voice belonged to the last person in this whole school—no, this whole state—no, on this planet—I wanted to see or hear from. I didn't want to turn around. Maybe if I ignored the irritating sound of Al Dutch's voice, he would go away.

"This . . . this is important," he said, kinda stuttering and uncool.

Yeah, his girlfriend was going to the hospital, and I regretted that. But had this been the first time she'd been physically assaulted? Maybe he'd done it before and we could pin this whole thing on him. At the end of the day, it was partly his fault that Cheryl had freaked out in the first place. And he'd better leave me alone because he didn't want me to get started on that. All she had to do was say he raped her, and I'd be right there testifying he had done it to me as well.

Instead of answering him, I tried walking away, but he grabbed my arm, and I screamed, "Let go!"

The cops were staring in our direction. The jerk quickly let my arm go. I didn't want him to touch me. I cringed.

"Can't you see she doesn't want to talk to you?" Sam said. "You've caused too much damage to my friends."

"I need to speak to her now, all right?" he said, placing his hand in Sam's face.

While Sam and Isha held him up, I walked away. I couldn't talk to him. There were no words he could say that I wanted to hear. I would rather listen to the police give us bad news about our chapter than stand there and listen to his bull. So that's what I did—walked over to the police.

"I would hate to have to arrest all these girls," the white officer said boldy to our black campus cop.

"Well, I don't know what to tell you," the campus police said, having our backs. "You have no evidence. These girls are being tight-lipped and not giving up any information."

"Well, she didn't get busted up by herself," the man with the prune face said, trying to scare us.

"Well, the method you're using isn't working. We're gonna head back over to my station and try to figure this out."

The city cop said, "And just let the girls go free?"

"We can handle this internally. Campus business. The ambulance has notified us, and the girl is breathing and doing fine. When she decides to talk and tell us who did this, you can come and get somebody, but right now you gotta let this go, sir."

"I'll be back," the city policeman said, frustrated as he walked out of the gym.

"Y'all need to talk, and y'all know you had no business having no party without no adviser. This is just dumb! Y'all know my wife is a Beta, so I'll do what I can, but a brother ain't losing his job. I don't think nobody can save you from this one," the campus officer yelled to us.

We all just looked around at each other. Cheryl was nowhere to be found. We were standing up for her, and she had abandoned us. This was horrible. What was up with her?

* * *

I didn't get two feet away from the crowd before Al Dutch approached me again. I just went off on him.

I screamed, "Why are you messing with me? You took everything I had, and then you blamed me for your actions. You made me feel like nothing, and now you stand here, on a horrible night for my chapter, wanting to make me feel worse. Go to the hospital and see about Meagan. Leave me alone!"

As soon as I turned to the left, he stepped in front of me. I had to do a double take for a second because it looked like he had water in his eyes. I knew Meagan looked bad; I'd seen her myself. There had been lots of blood, and her eyes had been swollen; she wasn't pretty. I thought he would just brush it off and leave her for somebody else, but yet he stood there, emotional and crying. I mean, was there something about their relationship I didn't know? Had she had a reason to go off on all us women—Ginger, Cheryl, me—because she and Al had something serious? And then reality hit. Why would I care about his tears? The police had said she was okay, so her life wasn't going to end. So what if he loved her? He had taken something from me, so he could go rot.

"Don't you get it? I really need to talk to you," he said, pulling on my shirt.

"Okay. Say what you gotta say right here," I said, moving away from his grip and standing near Alyx.

He leaned in and said, "No, this is serious. I need to speak with you alone. It's about my health."

Okay, now I was extra confused. His health? Why would he need to talk to me about his health? Other than the water in his eyes, he looked practically fine. He wasn't the one with the swollen face and blood gushing everywhere. Then it dawned on me; he probably had a disease, and he needed to talk to me about it. No!

I turned around and motioned for him to follow me. I didn't know where I was walking, and I didn't wanna be alone with him, but this was private, and I needed to be able to hear everything he had to say. There was still so much commotion going on at the dance. My chapter sorors were blaming each other, and everybody was encouraging the deejay to crank the party back up. We walked to the hallway for quiet space.

I turned and faced him, ready to hear what he had to say. Was it gonorrhea, herpes, syphilis, or what? He stood there like a lump of meat and said nothing. I just waited. I knew for a guy with an enormous ego, it would be difficult admitting his problem.

He finally looked away and blurted out, "I'm HIV positive. I don't know how long I've had it, so you might wanna go get yourself tested. Legally, I'm bound to tell you."

I was suddenly pounding his chest over and over, and he just sat there and took it. And now everything was making sense. Meagan had accused us of ruining things with Al Dutch. Had he told her? Did she know? Cheryl had become a zombie and lost it—did she know? And Ginger was nowhere to be found, and she never missed a party. Did she know?

Al Dutch finally left me there feeling hopeless again. I felt so empty. Was I HIV positive, too? Or, even worse, did I have full-blown AIDS coming my way? And if so, would my life be pointless?

BEND

I felt like a crowbar bent by a Sasquatch. Not broken, but definitely damaged. This was some of the worst news I had ever heard in my life. As much as I wanted Al Dutch to suffer for what he had put me through, I wouldn't have wished this on him, and I certainly didn't deserve it. I couldn't just wallow in my state of doom, so I picked myself up, wiped the tears from my weakened eyes, and began to search for Cheryl in the gym. I needed answers.

Isha tried to talk to me, but I pushed her right outta my way. I wasn't trying to be rude or hurt her feelings, but she wasn't who I was looking for. I needed to find someone who could relate to me at this very moment. I needed to find the person who could understand the weight of the world I was carrying on my shoulders.

When I reached the parking lot and searched for Cheryl's car, I realized I was outta luck. Sorors were coming up to me, asking what was wrong. I thought I was acting sane, but I guess my actions were a little sporadic. I was all over the place, and I could not find Cheryl anywhere I looked on campus.

Then the sky cracked open, and it started pouring down rain. As my tears also covered my face, I looked up to the sky, not caring if the lightning struck me or not. I was practically at death's door, so what did it matter anyway?

With a heart heavier than a zoo's largest elephant, I said, "Lord, this is too much for me to bear. HIV? Not me."

Trying to think where Cheryl could be, I got in my car and drove over to her apartment. I thought I knew the way, but I was sketchy on the directions. Cheryl was always so apprehensive about inviting us over. Shoot, I knew I didn't have much, but she always acted as though she didn't even have a bed to sleep on or something.

Sure enough, her beat-up-yet-still-running automobile was in front of the apartment. I got out of the car to bang on her door. Knock after knock, I got no answer, but I refused to leave.

"Cheryl, it's me, Cassidy. Please open up. I need to speak to you. It's urgent. It's not about the police. Let me in for just a second. I don't care about the place, Cheryl. This is important. If you care about me at all, open up," I pleaded, tired of beating on her door.

Finally, she answered. The hard, strong girl I was used to compared not one bit to the stranger who stood before me. Cheryl was trembling profusely. Her eyes looked like the eyes of someone who had been beaten rather than someone who had beat on someone.

"This isn't a good time, Cassidy," she said, looking at the ground. "Please leave me alone. Go."

When she tried to shut the door, I forced my way inside. Cheryl did not look happy, but, honestly, this was not a happy moment. She and I were in the same boat, sinking fast. We needed two minds to find a way to stay afloat.

"Al Dutch raped me at the beginning of the year," I told her. "He stopped me tonight and told me what was going on with him."

"You knew he was an animal, and you let me go out with him!" she screamed.

Not wanting to be attacked, I yelled back, "You and I weren't even tight then. And I didn't know how to talk to you about what I had gone through. Plus, you seemed so into Al Dutch. You never would have believed me, because you wanted to be with him. Besides, mentally, the incident tore me up. That's why I shut down earlier this year. That's why I had a breakdown. That's why I understand why you went off on Meagan tonight. Getting life-altering information dropped on you out of nowhere is a lot. We can all respond in so many different ways. I'm scared, Cheryl, and I just came by here to tell you that—"

"Tell me what, huh? That you're here for me? We're in the same boat now. A boat I could've been out of if you would've shared what kind of monster he was, but yet you just allowed me to continue seeing him. We both might be done, thanks to that fool. And though I'm so sorry about everything that happened with Meagan tonight, I just need you to leave, Cassidy. Some things you just can't fix. My aunt has AIDS, and if that's what we got headed toward us, that's a windy cycle of turmoil we can never get out of. And to know you could have prevented all this for me, but you didn't, makes me hate you as much as I hate Al Dutch."

As I stood on the other side of her closed door, I just felt worse. My stomach was all twisted up in knots. Question was, could I become untangled?

"Will you please talk to me and tell me what's going on?" Sam said to me when I got back to the apartment early in the morning. "I didn't know where you or Cheryl were, and I need some answers, Cass."

I couldn't have told her where I had been; I had no clue. After my tongue lashing from Cheryl, I had just driven around hoping, wishing, and praying that all that had gone on in the last eight hours was made up. A fairy tale. A dream waiting for me to wake up. But when I walked in the front door to see Sam standing there worried, I knew that wasn't the case. This was real, and I had to deal with it. Truth was, did I know how?

When I didn't respond, she started crying. "You can't break down again. You can't do this to me. I feel like I'm going crazy, unable to help you, unable to make it better. I can't get Cheryl to return my calls, and now you're acting weird. Isha and I have been praying you'd walk through the door. I asked her to come over because I was worried."

"Where is she?" I asked.

Sam pointed to my door. "She's asleep in your bed-room."

"No, I'm awake. I hear you guys talking," Isha called out from my room.

"She hasn't said anything," Sam said. "Come out here and help me get some answers. Shoot, Isha, I'm tired, too, but we need to know what's going on."

I realized I had sent my two girls into worry. But by telling them everything, wouldn't it be worse? Isha came to the door and rubbed Sam's back. They were united, ready to get me to open up. Looking deep into their concerned eyes, I knew that telling them would make it better. Sam would be there to rationalize all this. Isha would be there to give me a spiritual perspective.

I took both of their hands and said, "This is heavy, y'all, okay, and I need you to be strong for me." They nodded, so I continued. "There's a reason they tell girls not to sleep around with men."

"Are you pregnant?" Sam asked.

"You're dating a pastor. What do you mean 'sleep around'?" Isha said.

"Wait a minute. What pastor?" Sam said, seemingly irritated that I hadn't told her about my new beau.

"No, guys. Listen, this is before Konner, okay? Sam, I'm not pregnant, even though that would be better than the news I'm about to share."

"So then what are you talking about?" Isha asked.

Sam looked nervous. She knew this had something to do with the rape. More tears strolled down her face. This was hard. I was hurting for me, and now I knew my girls were gonna be crushed hearing this.

I took a deep breath and said, "Isha, I never really told you what drew me to the church and why I connected with the sermon the first night you took me to your youth service. But a similar experience happened to me. I was raped by a student on campus."

"It was that crazy Al Dutch," Sam said with fire in her eyes.

"Did you report it? Why is he still walking around like he is the big, bad wolf on campus? I remember he wanted to talk to you tonight. What did he want?" Isha questioned.

"He told me he has HIV."

"Oh, my gosh. No, Cass, no. Wait, he's been with Cheryl, too," Sam said as I nodded.

We all stood there in silence, but we didn't need any words. The fact that they didn't leave me, stayed by my side, and continued holding my hands let me know I had the extra strength I needed to make it through.

Later that night I was resting. Well, I was trying to anyway. It was actually hard to sleep. I was sort of lying there looking out of my apartment window.

I looked up at the sky and asked, "Lord, do You care about me? Did I find You too late? Am I a lost cause? Can I be fixed? Will You help me?"

There were so many unanswered questions. I felt like I couldn't hear God speak at all. There was no way I could be mad at Him when I was the one who had been promiscuous.

A knock at my door interrupted my thoughts. I had appreciated Sam and Isha's help, but this was my battle. I had told them earlier that I was fine. I had gotten myself into this, and I would get myself out, even if "out" meant I would soon be dead. We all had to go that road eventually. I just wished I could do it over or tell other young girls my story so they wouldn't end up scared like me.

The knock came again. I just wanted to scream out to them to give me some time alone. I figured if I didn't answer the knocks, the person would go away. I figured wrong.

"Come in," I called out to the door after the third tap. When I looked up it was Konner Black looking so handsome and regal in jeans and a sweater. I was so used to seeing him decked out in suits that seeing him dressed all casual and cool made my heart skip a beat.

He said, "Look, I just like being honest with people. Now, I know you weren't expecting me, but I did call your cell. You didn't pick up."

"It's off somewhere. Now is not a good—" He put his fingers to my lips.

"Shhh!" he said. "I know you wanna be alone, but I got word from Isha that you may need my shoulder."

"What did she tell you?" I asked uneasily.

"She just said you need a friend. You might need someone to pray with you. I know when we left last time it wasn't on the best of terms, but like I told you then, I'm fond of you, and I meant that. If you need me, I wanna be here."

Was this guy a sign telling me the Lord did care? Was Konner the boost of help I needed to brighten my day? There was no way I could tell him, and I hoped Isha hadn't. I'd be too embarrassed.

I walked over to my window. I couldn't hold back the emotion. Konner came over and placed his arm around my waist. He was so comforting as he just held me and allowed me to cry in his arms.

He kissed me on the cheek and asked, "Do you wanna talk about it?"

I realized that if I did open up, we would never be a couple. But I didn't want to do to him what Al Dutch had done to me. I mean, Al had been with me under false pretenses; some girl had probably already told him she was HIV positive—or some guy, knowing his wild behind. He had probably thought he was resilient to the disease, and it would just bounce off his back, like he had never come in contact. Now he had put me and who knows how many others at risk.

Yet there I stood in the arms of a gentleman who cared deeply for me—so much so that he wanted to save a special part of himself for me until God said it was right. To make sure I was never tempted again. The idea of me being HIV positive and the possibility of me giving it to Konner made me jerk out his arms.

"What's wrong with you? Just talk to me. I promise we can work it out. I'm not gonna judge you, Cassidy," Konner said. "Isha told me nothing."

Very upset, I shouted, "Earlier in the year I was raped by some creep, okay?"

He said, "Well, we can deal with that. Did you know who it was? Have you reported it? We can get through this."

"No, we can't. He just told me tonight that he's HIV positive!" I yelled and just lost control.

He didn't leave. He held me close and said, "Listen. Cassidy, it's okay. This is bad news, but I'm not going to allow you to be broken. You can cry and get it out, whatever you want. We're gonna work through this. Cassidy, you're too strong to break. God brought you this far down this dark, curvy road. Things will straighten out. He won't leave you here in the bend."

GRIPE

"I can't believe this is happening! What did I do to deserve this? He violated me in the highest degree. I didn't wanna have sex with him. He just took it. He had his way with me, Konner! I know you're gonna think I'm just another fast girl. No guy would take that from me if I wasn't leading him on, sending all the wrong signals," I said to the guy who had been kind enough to come to my side and comfort me.

I walked to the other side of the room, humiliated and bummed out that I had to involve a guy like Konner, who was too good to be with me. I couldn't expect him to stay.

"Come on, Cassidy. You gotta know that all guys out there aren't jerks. It's taking all of the Holy Spirit in me not to go looking for this punk and bust him up." He placed his arms around me and said, "I know this is difficult. You can vent to me as much as you want. Now that we know what we're dealing with, let's develop a plan."

Okay, he was saying this "we" thing, and I felt real snug and secure in his muscular arms, but I was still uneasy. I couldn't allow him to be my hero in all this. I'd been a victim, and the only way I was going to feel good about myself again was if I dealt with this alone.

"You know what?" I said, pushing away and changing my tone to a stern one. "While I appreciate you coming over here, and I certainly needed to talk, I am not all right with this whole we're-gonna-make-a-plan thing. Maybe you could just pray for me or whatever. I will leave it up to God's doing. I will sit back and let time determine how I feel. If nothing changes, I should be good because Al Dutch doesn't fully have AIDS yet. I should be okay."

His eyes squinted, and his face held a disgusted look. "That's just crazy!" he blurted out, not even caring about what I'd said. "So you're saying you're not gonna get tested and you're just gonna wait and see how you feel? I can only imagine that this is not easy to deal with, but you gotta have medical proof that you are okay. I believe in my heart that you are, but you have to want to do this for yourself. Be responsible for yourself about the situation, finally."

"Finally!" I remarked, becoming defensive. "Are you saying I wasn't responsible before?"

"No, I'm not saying that at all. I'm just saying you could finally put all this worry to rest. Don't wonder and worry needlessly when there is testing that can be done to determine your fate. If you are HIV positive, there are meds out there for you. The earlier you find out, the quicker you can get treated. Don't be careless, Cassidy. Go out and get tested right away."

"You know what? If I'm so careless, this is my life. Maybe I was crazy enough to let you in. Please get out because I don't want to hear your complaints, suggestions, or sermons about how I should live my life."

"Ain't no need for you to sit in here and talk about anybody else," Loni said to Torian as the two of them literally talked about me behind my back.

The chapter meeting was about to start, and a part of me didn't even wanna stay. I knew the whole school knew about Al Dutch and what was going on with him. It had been only two days, but bad news traveled quicker than an e-mail sent over the Internet.

Al Dutch had packed up, moved out, and been transferred. All everybody really knew was he was HIV positive and had admitted to the Centers for Disease Control that he had slept with more than twenty women in the last six months. Because I had just sat down at our chapter meeting, I wasn't sure if Torian and Loni were talking about me specifically or what, but if they were, it was going to be on.

"Girl, please!" Torian said to Loni. "I was not that dumb to be with the fool."

"Whatever. Both you and her need to go to the doctor. I don't believe you and Al Dutch didn't go all the way."

"I'm telling you we didn't. I didn't sleep with him. He got overly aggressive, trying to get me to do this and that, and I socked him right in the nose. The punk wasn't that big and bad then when I threatened to use my mace on his behind," Torian said.

"You never told me that," Loni said, laughing. "You came back and said everything was great."

Torian said, "It *was* great. Not great in bed, but great that I didn't have to be violated. At least now I'm glad I didn't go through with being with that slick-talking, disease-carrying dog."

At that exact second my eyes welled up. Just hearing Torian say that all she did was give a little resistance and Al Dutch had backed off made me wonder why I hadn't done the same. Why hadn't I hit him, punched him, kicked him, and jabbed him? Why did I lay there and take it? Too late for all those *why nots.*

So I took a deep breath and remembered what Konner had said. It was what it was, and I had to deal with it. I just wasn't certain about testing. Yeah, I had thought about it long and hard over the last forty-eight hours since I had pushed a good man out of my life. Truth was, I was scared that the test would come back positive. Yeah, we were all gonna die one day, but to know my time may be shorter rather than longer was extremely un-settling. This whole ordeal made me feel like I was wear-ing size-A panty hose when I really needed a D; there were rips, holes, and tears everywhere in my life. Was there any relief in sight?

All of a sudden Cheryl came busting in the door, and there was a whole bunch of buzz in the room. Isha and Sam weren't too far behind her, and they came and sat beside me. Cheryl walked up to Malloy and Alyx, who were at the front table. They gave her a chance to speak.

"I just wanna say that y'all been doing a lot of talking about me and other females in this chapter who were victims of Al Dutch. I know that I put you guys in an awkward situation, and now you know why I lost my mind. I had just gotten some horrible news, but that was no excuse to keep beating that girl. But I want to address that we talk about sisterhood, and if you go out with a guy who forces himself on you and you're not comfortable telling anyone else, you should be able to come to your sisters so we won't repeat your mistakes. I know some people have to learn some things for themselves, but at least give us the information and allow us to decide. I might be dying because one of our sorors decided to withhold life-threatening information. And because of her my life may not be spared. Are we really sisters in here, y'all?" Cheryl dashed out of the room.

I could barely sit there and stand hearing all the rumblings around. If I could have, I would have returned my Beta Gamma Pi card because I certainly felt like I wasn't a part of the bond. Even though I had kept my experiences with Al Dutch to myself, not wanting to hurt anyone, now it didn't seem like the right choice, and I had hurt someone a great deal. On top of everything else I was carrying, this had to be the worst. But what could I do but own up to it? I couldn't change it. Or could I? I had to tell the chapter I was the person who had betrayed Cheryl. I could do it.

* * *

"All right, sorors. Calm down," Malloy said. "We need a point of order. Everybody can't talk at the same time."

A senior soror on the first line, who I didn't know, stood up and said, "Whoever did this to her needs to apologize to us right now."

"Some things just need to be left alone," Torian called out from behind her.

"No, it doesn't need to be left alone," the soror continued. "Beta Gamma Pi is founded on Christian principles, and we keep forgetting that."

"Forget the Christian thing to do and focus on the sisters. This is a sorority, not a church," Torian retorted.

What did they want me to do, replay in detail how Al Dutch had raped me? Go through all that again and let them know I had kept it to myself because I didn't want to be mentally damaged forever? Plus, I remembered the night I had brought this whole awful mess on myself—every girl in the room had been drooling to be with him. Yeah, I guess I needed to stand and set them straight. Had I told them then, they would have still wanted him. That's what the real issue was. We needed to truly trust each other and not have to learn everything the hard way.

Just when I was about to stand and admit it was me who had hurt Cheryl—and confess that I was also one of Al Dutch's pawns—Isha stood and said, "It was me. I heard at the church that Al Dutch was HIV positive. One of the new members at the church came out and told everything. I knew Cheryl liked him. The problem was I didn't know so many other people in here did, too," she said as she looked over at me. "I wasn't sure it was true, and I definitely thought Cheryl would hate me for getting in her business. I should have said what I knew. I ruined her life."

"That was dumb," Torian said from behind us. "You would have wanted to know."

"Yeah, you should've said something," Loni uttered.

"Shut up!" I yelled to the both of them. "By the grace of God, you ain't better than any of us in here, Torian. A lot of this mess we're in right now is because you're so strong-willed. You think your way is the only way that's right. We're in a sorority; that means we're all equal. This is not a dictatorship, and this is not Torian's world. You wanted to let a great adviser go, and right now we're conducting business out of order. So don't say what is dumb. And, dang it, Loni, you need to quit following her, just like the rest of us do."

"Point taken, Cassidy. Everybody just have a seat. This is a lot for us to deal with," Alyx stated, standing between us so no one would fight.

"I'm not gonna sit here and let some neophyte call me out like that. I got some stuff I wanna say, and I'm not gonna sit down right now," Torian said.

"Yes, you are," Malloy called out, banging the gavel.

"Girl, just sit," Loni said, yanking her down, obviously knowing she did need to quit following Torian and stand up to her sometimes.

"We are a Christian-based organization," Malloy said, "and we need to deal with this like a higher power is holding us accountable. We need to get on to the business at hand, and that's where our chapter stands."

All of a sudden Torian pushed me. "No, we need to

deal with this right now because I'm not gonna allow this girl to come in here and tell me what to do. You might be going through a lot, Cassidy—you and Cheryl, and I hate that. But I mean, I was smart enough to leave the fool alone, but don't come in here and take it out on me because I didn't sleep with the guy. You think I don't have any feelings?"

"Nobody's saying that," Loni said to her.

"You need to keep your hands off my friend," Sam said to Torian.

Everyone was waiting, even Torian, to see how I would respond. "I'm dealing with a lot right now, Torian. I overheard some of your conversation with Loni, and I am so thankful that you had the strength not to be victimized like I was. If it would make you feel better to hit me because I told you the truth, then you need to be a woman, quit all these threats, and hit me. Isha wasn't the only one who let Cheryl down. Everyone has been talking about me and Al Dutch, but the truth is, Al Dutch raped me. I was too fast, and everybody knew it. My reputation forced my roommate and I to keep quiet, and it drove me crazy. Because I kept quiet, Cheryl got with him, and now both of us are in a mess. I'm upset right now with myself. With you, there is no gripe."

PURPOSE

"Thanks for agreeing to ride with me, Cassidy," Alyx said as we headed to Little Rock to see her boyfriend's play the next day.

He had written, directed, and produced a musical that had gotten funded and was traveling around the southeast. When she'd called me last night and asked if I'd ride with her so she wouldn't have to make the trip alone, I agreed—so I could get out of my world and step into somebody else's.

Alyx Cruz wasn't the type of person who gave lectures, so I didn't think I would be ridiculed. But she did have a way of putting in her two cents. I knew she really cared about me because she had made sure I made the line months back, knowing that most of the girls weren't really feeling me. I knew she'd had to go to bat, call in favors, and stick out her neck with her sorors to get me voted in. Realizing that, I knew if she said anything to me now, it would be because she had reason behind it and a point. She would say whatever she'd say to better me because she cared. However, I did prefer to ride in silence.

Without being forceful—she saw I was in deep thought—she said, "Wish there were some things you could go back and change?"

I knew she wasn't being funny, that she wasn't putting me down, but she was calling a spade a spade. I just looked out the window. I wasn't trying to be disrespectful, and I certainly didn't want to tell her to shut up, but now I was in a predicament. What good would it be to rehash what should have been buried?

Even though she could see I was uneasy with the conversation, she surprisingly kept going—she didn't back off. So I knew her motives were pure. She wanted to talk me through my gloom.

With one hand on the steering wheel, she used the other to touch my shoulder. "My heart's breaking hearing about this whole Al Dutch thing you're caught up in, but rumor has it a lot of you girls are afraid to go get a test. Not wanting to find out if you're afflicted with this thing or not. I'm not your mother, Cassidy. I don't even have mine anymore," she said, reminding me of last year when we all got word that one of the Beta's mom had passed; I had been saddened to find out it was hers.

Alyx had been new to the school. She'd transferred last year, but she had such style, such charisma, such grace—she was one of those people who has it going on—and I wanted to be like her. It was easy to get caught up in her hype because you could believe what she set out to do. She was out to make it happen. Yeah, she was a little wild, too, and that was probably why she liked me. Books weren't her thing when she'd first come to Western Smith, but she'd buckled down and gotten it together. She'd blossomed in front of our eyes.

So I believed her when she said, "I haven't done everything right either. Served some time in jail last year for a mistake I made, almost could've killed somebody driving drunk. But God gave me another chance. You got to face the music and know what you're dealing with and know what kind of chance you have if—"

"What kind of life will I have, Alyx," I said, "if I'm dying?"

"We're all dying. We all got one foot in the grave. The more you live, though, the more you learn, and the more you learn, the more you're expected to do with that knowledge. If you know you need to take certain medicines right now to give you even more life on this earth, wouldn't you want to be taking that medicine? I mean, it's a no-brainer. An idiot wants medicine when he's sick. Do nothing, and your odds of fulfilling your destiny diminish because you can't do nothing for God, Alpha chapter, yourself, or anybody if you're not here. And if you do nothing more than spend your days telling other young women about the scary incident, you need to live many days to tell that message. I know deep down inside my heart that there's much more you want to do than even that. But again, if you do nothing more than help somebody else not go the way you went, you got to take care of yourself. You got to not be afraid. You got to step out on faith and find out your fate."

I took in her words. We enjoyed the rest of our time

and went to see a great play. She was a little bummed because she couldn't spend that much time with her guy. We headed on back to our school, but something was different in me. I was now open to facing my fears. Now God and I were going to have to conquer those fears together.

"What do you mean, we got to go to the President's office for a big meeting?" I said to Samantha as she delivered the scary news to me the next morning.

"I don't know all the details. I just know they're investigating whether or not they're going to keep Alpha chapter on campus, and, you know, we're already on probation, so it does not look good. I think we're going to lose our chapter forever, for good," Sam said dramatically and with good reason.

I rationalized, "Why would he do that? We do so much good for the community. Just the Betas being on campus is a big deal. We're leaders. We make a difference. Why would Western Smith want to lose us?"

"Why wouldn't they? When you break the rules and you think you can decide things on your own, sometimes you have to be broken, dismantled altogether." Sam sat down on the couch and put her head in her hands.

"So, what, you agree with this decision?" I plopped down beside her.

"No, no, it's not that I agree, but I'm not naive. It's not like I think we don't deserve to be called into his office to even entertain this. I wish it wasn't so, but we have strict rules and guidelines for what we should and shouldn't do. No parties of any kind for a year. We were supposed to do only public service stuff, and, boy, did we break that. We should have listened to you, Cass."

"Yep, and everything we do we're supposed to have an adviser on campus, and we've certainly broken that rule," I told her, still bitter that they'd let a great lady go who had cared deeply for us. "And we weren't supposed to cause any strife on campus but only do good, and we had the campus police and the city police called out to break up one of our own from fighting another girl. Do we even know how Meagan is?"

"She's on *your* dance team," Sam said to me as if I should know.

"You're right. I guess after all that stuff with Al Dutch, nobody wants to go dancing. We haven't had to practice since the competition has been called off. Honestly, I've been in my own world."

"I'm sure the President knows how Meagan's doing."

"So what are we supposed to do? What are we supposed to say when we're in there?"

"I think it's just a meeting to listen," Sam said.

The President wanted to meet with all the active Betas, and he had given us only a twelve-hour notice. Hayden Grant, his niece and our former Chapter President, didn't live too far away, and we were shocked to see her at the meeting. After all, Hayden was in graduate school, but she spoke to us all as we were in the President's waiting area. A girl who looked like her twin was standing next to her. We were all waiting on an introduction. Nosey Betas, I guess.

"Don't be looking crazy, like, what am I doing here. This is my sister, Hailey—she's a freshman this year, and my uncle told her about this meeting, so she called me," Hayden said, with disappointment on her face.

Malloy took the lead and said, "Hey, Hailey, nice to meet you."

Hayden stood in her way. Her body language let us know this wasn't a social call. The Hailey girl didn't seem at all shaken with the fact that she'd ratted us out to her big sister. If she wanted to pledge one day, the chances of that now happening were lessened. Shoot, that was if we even still had a chapter on campus to deal with.

Hayden said, "Forget introductions, we're here about business. I thought you guys cared about our chapter. I thought you all wanted to make a difference. Now you all are on the verge of losing it. You must think this chapter is a cat with nine lives or something. Well, you're wrong. This may very well be the last straw. We got kicked off when I was President. My uncle has to abide by what the state says. This is not about blood or family. This is about what's right and what's wrong, and knowing him the way I do, he's going to want to hear more than a sob story. It's going to take a move of his heart not to immediately kick you guys off campus for good right now. I tried to get in touch with him, but he wouldn't return my call. But I just wanted to tell you guys, look deep inside your souls, and whatever it is you're really thinking, let it come out. He'll see through the phoniness, the sobs. Give him a reason to care."

We all hugged her, and she and her sister left. Soon after, the secretary came out and told us to go into the President's conference room. Most of us had to stand. We let the upperclassmen and officers sit at the table.

President Webb walked in a few moments later, and he cut right to chase. "Listen, I've got a lot of heat on me right now by the board of this school and some upset parents that Beta Gamma Pi does not need to be on this campus. I called this meeting to hear from you and find out what is going on with you young ladies that you can't understand to stay in compliance. Do you want to still have a presence here?"

"Sir, if I may," Malloy said. "As the Chapter President, we know we've let the school down, but the circumstances were beyond our control."

He looked at her real crazily. She had to be real with him, like his niece had said. Malloy couldn't blow this for us.

He said, "I think you girls are very smart. You are in control of everything you do. Please don't feed me bull."

"Love got in the way," I stood up and said, trying to shoot from the heart. "It made us a little bit crazy. President Webb, a lot of us got mixed up with the wrong crowd, and those crazy emotions made us lose our minds, but, sir, this organization was created for good. If you search deep inside each of our souls, good is all we want to do."

"Well, someone, if not the whole organization, is going to have to pay. And I understand it from the police that no one wanted to give up the young lady's name who inflicted all the violence. I'm going to give you guys thirty days to give me a name so that person can be expelled, or Alpha chapter's gone. You young people think you can do anything you want to do and there are no consequences. I don't care if love got in the way or a Mack truck struck you and made you lose your mind, there is a correct way to handle any tough situation, and sometimes taking it into your own hands can only lead to trouble. The Betas don't rule this campus—at the moment, I do. So I'll see you in thirty days, and we'll find out what's going to happen with the Betas."

The President got up and walked out. He had spoken, and the chapter was extremely torn. Loyalty or survival—both couldn't coexist. At the end of the day, what were the Betas of Alpha chapter at Western Smith College going to stand for? The clock was ticking.

All week we'd been arguing as a chapter. Some wanted one thing, others wanted another. Was it about protecting our sister, or was it about protecting ourselves? Would we even be a sisterhood if we sold Cheryl out? Or how could we be a sisterhood if we weren't even on campus?

I felt like I had already let Cheryl down by not telling her what Al Dutch had done to me, by trying not to be embarrassed or by feeling people wouldn't believe me. Wanting to just keep my business to myself. I hadn't given my sister all she needed then, and I just could not do that again.

Torian and Loni, on the other hand, were ready for Cheryl to step forward and say what she did, and if she wasn't going to do it, they were ready to. It was like Cheryl was AWOL. Sorors said she hadn't been to class; no one had seen her around campus. My roommate was one of her best friends, and she wasn't taking Sam's calls. It was too weird to imagine.

That next weekend, we went to the Founders' Day luncheon in Conway, Arkansas. Being at my first Founders' Day was something exciting. Betas from across the state were dressed in white for the occasion. Every five years we'd honor another founder. This year was the time to honor soror Lizzie Mae Perry.

They say she had been a maverick on campus who had believed in Christ from the start and would not become a part of the organization if He wasn't a part of it. Though she'd proclaimed the gospel as a collegiate, she hadn't been holier than thou. She'd been in an abusive relationship and had prayed so much that her husband had turned into a pastor. The motto she'd left on us was "God loves you despite yourself. Don't give up on yourself, but see Christ in your heart and strive to be like Him."

As we lit purple candles that day, symbolizing the royalty we are a part of—because we were children of the King—it was like I was rededicating my life to God all over again. I got a better understanding that Beta Gamma Pi was much larger than the Alpha chapter. Interacting with other Betas in our state let me know the importance of our causes. If we stood as one, we could do anything.

A little later, after we'd finished the plated meal of Alfredo chicken, assorted spring vegetables, and rice pilaf, the state coordinator came to the mic and made a riveting speech. "There is so much our sorority is supposed to do for this world. We're supposed to fight for worthwhile causes. We're supposed to help those who can't help themselves. We're supposed to leave our mark and do the best job we can, but, sorors, we can't do it alone. If we count on just ourselves, we're going to fall short. We need the Holy Spirit living inside each of us to work, to show us the way, to guide our footsteps, and to keep us out of harm. Sorors, Beta Gamma Pi is bigger than your school, your chapter, and the state. As our founder Lizzie Mae Perry knew deep in her heart, Beta Gamma Pi is successful only if God is in the middle of it. So I ask you to check yourselves today. Are you living for God? Are you being a Beta that He is proud of? Because when He's walking in you and through you, then and only then are you a Beta with purpose."

BEST

"I really think Konner is the right man for you, girl," Isha said to me after the luncheon. Isha, Sam, and I were trying to come up with a way to get Cheryl out of her predicament and Sam had just gone to the bathroom.

I was very caught off guard by the statement. It was kinda ironic, though. I had been thinking about Konner a lot over the past few days. He hadn't called or come by unexpectedly like he had the last time I'd thrown him out. I couldn't blame him at all. That day I had told him to leave when he'd been on my case about getting an HIV test; I had treated him so badly if I were him I wouldn't wanna be bothered with me either, let alone be in a relationship with me. All he did was extend kindness, care, and concern, and all I did was give him the cold shoulder, making him feel like I didn't need him in my life. And that was far from the truth.

"Hello? Earth to Cassidy. You here, girl?" Isha said.

But I wasn't listening. I was trying to visualize Konner holding me tight, telling me everything was going to be okay, and me kissing him, feeling good inside. But that dream was too far gone and stupid. I could possibly kill him if I had what I was afraid to find out about.

As I thought of Konner, it became clear that I'd made a mistake. Though he was not college educated, he certainly was intellectual, philosophical, and intelligent. He was a man who loved God more than he loved himself. A man who understood that people had tough backgrounds, imperfections, and drama. A man who saw good in other people and a man who saw good in me. Being around him made me feel better. Thinking about him made me happy. But dumb me had sent him away.

"You care about him, too. I see it in your face," Isha said.

"It doesn't matter what I want. He deserves better than me," I said.

"He doesn't care about, about . . ." Isha looked away, unable to conjure up the words.

"What, the disease?" I said. "Sure, he doesn't care about that now, but what if I have it? Would he want a girlfriend who's HIV positive?"

"He's a good man, Cassidy. He's trying to go about doing things the right way."

"I've never really had a boyfriend I could share my life's story with, but Konner was so caring. I didn't know what to do with his love. I was trying to push things a little too far, messing up his walk with God. Maybe all this turmoil I'm dealing with is because I didn't respect that."

"You should let him be the judge of what he wants to put up with or deserves to be around. I see him all the time, walking around our church youth group, and he asks me if you're okay."

"He deserves much better than me, though, Isha," I said to her.

"Well, the heart loves who the heart loves," Isha responded, clutching her chest. "And you ain't as bad as you think."

"Who loves who? That preacher man?" Sam asked as she walked back from the bathroom. "If that's who you two are gabbing about, then, girl, that man does love you. That day you kicked him out, he was a lost soul. I saw him sitting outside our place when I stepped out to get some milk, and he was pretty much in tears. I saw him quickly wipe his eyes when he saw me."

"He was probably sad from the news I told him. He wasn't upset because we were over." I tried convincing my girls. "That was it, right?"

"Maybe," Sam said. "But I don't think so."

"It was probably both. You know, just his emotions mixed together. He is a sensitive and emotional man who preaches and speaks the Word passionately. But all I'm saying is give him a call," Isha said.

"Okay. Well, the waiters are waiting to clear the room. Plus, enough about me. What are we going to do about Cheryl? I feel like I'm being so hypocritical, trying to lift her spirits and get her to quit being so isolated when I know exactly how she feels. This is some scary stuff," I said as the three of us walked out of the grand hotel.

When we got in Sam's car, she said, "We're still a family, and we're not gonna back away from what scares any of us. You're not going to have to be strong by yourself. Cheryl's not going to have to be strong by herself."

"Yep," Isha said, leaning up from the backseat and soothing my shoulder with her touch. "We are all in this together. You and Cheryl are not going to go through this alone."

It wasn't a good day for Beta Gamma Pi. The thirty days weren't even up, and the Regional Coordinator had paid us an unexpected visit to speak to us. I guess I was supposed to care and be on my best behavior, listening and being attentive, but my attention was elsewhere. I was at my wit's end trying to figure out how I was gonna get through to Cheryl. No matter how much of an effort Sam, Isha, and I tried to put through, she wanted nothing to do with us.

Konner was kinda in the same *leave me alone* category. I had taken Isha's advice and called him twice but had gotten no answer or returned calls. I texted him repeatedly one whole day while I was in class, and still no response. I hoped he wouldn't leave me hanging, but yet he was. I had even gone by the church, but he wasn't there. I left a message with his secretary telling him to call me, but that effort didn't bring the results I wanted either.

So now I was in the mindset of just leaving it alone. I had done everything I could to try to apologize and let him know, if nothing more, that I wanted him in my life as a friend, a minister, or a personal counselor. I didn't have to be a rocket scientist, astronaut, or scientific engineer to realize he clearly wanted to be left alone.

Realizing Konner was out the picture, I focused back on what the Regional Coordinator was saying. "Some of you are looking around and not taking this seriously, but let me be real with you. The school has contacted the sorority, and you ladies are under major investigation. Not only are you in trouble with the school, but the sorority has to look at how we're gonna take action from all this. You know you are not supposed to conduct an activity without an adviser present. Worse than that, no one gave approval to dismiss her. After your vote to dismiss her, the state director and I contacted her to understand why you all removed her, and she's been vague—meaning I recognize there is a good chance she caught you all doing something illegal. You all did not go through the proper procedures. I was not advised, and the National President didn't know. You can't just remove someone because you feel she's not capable. Then you guys are playing maverick by standing up for one of you who possibly needs some serious help, if she beat up a young lady like that. We got word that the other girl is pressing charges, and if you guys don't understand what probation means and that you were to have a squeaky-clean year, y'all might have to be the first to go down in history for destroying this Alpha chapter because of your foolishness."

The room was more silent than a graveyard. All my chapter sorors looked uneasy. They weren't having to deal with the possibility of losing their lives to AIDS, but it was highly probable they were losing their letters. Now they felt like I did—scared to death.

The stern Regional Coordinator continued. "It seems your chapter is more about hazing, boasting, and partying. Actually, Grand Chapter is not about any of those things at all. We wear our letters with pride, but we don't have to boast and brag about who we are. People see our work based on our deeds, not on our words. But when you conduct horrific actions, like break what our policies say by getting rid of someone because she's holding you accountable for being the best collegiate you can be, some things have to change. If the whole chapter isn't suspended, quite a lot of you will be. From this moment on, you guys will not have any activities. And the only way I will consider a recommendation to the National President for this chapter not to be removed is if you comply with the school to come clean and make the girl who fought come forward. You must also get your adviser, Dr. Garnes, to serve with you all again. She is not your ex-adviser, because we did not grant your request to terminate her service."

"But we don't want her!" Torian yelled, and Loni yanked her back in her seat. Other sorors screamed out, "Shhh!"

Angrily, the Regional Coordinator said, "Yeah, you all better quiet down, whoever that is, because this is not about what you all want. Grand Chapter knows what is best and what is needed. If you can't comply, no more Alpha chapter. That is definitely not a threat—it's a promise. Handle your business."

As Sam and I arrived back at our place from the meeting with the Regional Coordinator, both of us were stunned. With eyes wide open, as if we'd just witnessed a historical event or something, we were shocked to see Cheryl perched at our front door. Sam immediately went over and hugged her tight. The grip wasn't reciprocated, but as I looked at Cheryl and saw her eyes tear up, I knew she appreciated it.

"Hey, Sam, I need to talk to Cassidy," Cheryl said, staring at me with a face I could not read.

"Sure, girl," Sam responded as she came out of the hug, straightening up Cheryl's shirt that had been messed up during the embrace.

Before unlocking the door and going inside, Sam peered over at me as if to say *Please take care of my friend. Please don't say anything to make Cheryl upset.* I nodded at Sam, signaling to her that I understood.

When Sam was inside and Cheryl and I shared the privacy of the outside air, she said, with no emotion, "I need you to go with me."

"Okay," I said, without knowing where we were going. As Cheryl moved toward her car, I thought about the fact that the chick may still hate my guts, so I wisely asked, "Where?"

She walked back to me and got really close, so close that I could feel her breath on my skin as she said, "I owe you a big apology. I've been so mad at you and others in the chapter for not telling me what kind of monster Al Dutch was, when all I had to do was live by God's word and keep my legs closed in the first place. I wouldn't be in such a predicament."

Hearing her apologize was tough to take. I still felt responsible and didn't want to be off the hook. However, I knew, to connect with her again, she had to forgive me. Deep down I knew I was wrong for showing Al Dutch I was willing to give it up at the party that night; so, too, was Cheryl ultimately responsible for giving in to him herself.

Cheryl continued, "Well, now it's time for me to face the music. I've gotten so many e-mails, phone calls, and texts about you not wanting to get tested. Now it's time to go. We both may be infected, maybe both not, and maybe only one, I don't know. But we need to know, Cassidy. As many people offered to go with me to find out what was going on, I knew there was one person who understood how uneasy all this feels. And if you came all the way to my crib that night you found out, I need to help you through this as well. I guess what I'm saying is, if you can come to me and let me know that your heart is breaking and that we are both carrying the weight of the world on our shoulders, I know now that I can't care only about myself—I have to care about you, too."

Cheryl's words were profound. We did need to get through this together. Like a person with a horrible toothache dreading to go to the dentist, so, too, had I been putting off going to get the HIV test.

"Let's go deal with our consequences. We both have to do this," she said as she gripped my hand.

Without hesitating I said, "Okay. But I need to make one more stop."

Cheryl said, "Cool."

I had Cheryl drive to Ginger's dorm. She and I hadn't talked in a couple weeks. She had called and left messages, but just like Cheryl had done with me, I hadn't returned them. Ginger's support and concern had suddenly sunk in.

Cheryl stayed in the car, and I went up to talk to Ginger. I told her where the two of us were going. She said she had an appointment for the following week, but why put it off? She grabbed her purse, and the three of us were off to the clinic where Al Dutch had been tested.

As we sat in the waiting room, none of us spoke. Ginger couldn't stop fidgeting, and Cheryl couldn't stop crying. I couldn't stop praying.

Silently I chatted with God. *Lord, right now the three of us are getting ready to go through with this HIV test. I know You're always on Your game, but today is a big day for Ginger, Cheryl, and me. Could You help us out and only give us news that is best?*

GRATEFUL

The next two weeks were brutal as I waited for the results from my HIV test. Thank goodness I had school projects and sorority drama to occupy my mind. Otherwise I would have lost it again. Every day I went to the mailbox, nervous, to see if there was an envelope from the clinic, and I was relieved when there wasn't so I wouldn't have to deal with the outcome one way or the other.

But one particular day after I put in my key and opened the mailbox for our apartment, I felt a panic attack coming on when I saw the clinic's name at the top of the letterhead. PERSONAL AND CONFIDENTIAL were stamped on the outside of the white envelope for Cassidy Cross. The time to find out my fate was now.

Also keeping me sane was the fact that I had been studying God's word. If there was one thing I had learned it was that God won't give you more than you can bear. Believing in my faith, I tore into the envelope. Now was the time for me to deal with it. Whatever it was I had to face, I wouldn't have to do it alone.

Slowly I read the words: **Cassidy Cross, you have tested negative for the HIV virus. Please be advised that we recommend two more sets of testing over the next six months.**

The letter had more instructions, but I needed to speak to the doctor to make sure I was cleared for now. Immediately rushing to the phone to dial the clinic, I got on my knees as the phone rang. God had done me a favor, and before I did anything else, I had to express my gratitude.

"Lord," I called out, "thank you, thank you, thank you. I've learned a big lesson. I know I'm not out of the woods, but thank you, Lord. It feels like a mountain has been moved from my heart."

"Dr. Oak's office. May I help you?" the lady said, cutting off my praise.

Gathering my thoughts, I said, "Yes, this is Cassidy Cross. I just had some HIV testing done."

"Yes, Ms. Cross, this is Nurse Stevens. How may I help you?" the sweet voice said.

"I just received my letter."

"Great, do you have any questions about the results?"

"Yes, may I speak to the doctor?"

Nurse Stevens said, "She has just come out from seeing a patient. If you hold just a second, I'll get her on the line."

Moments later, the doctor said, "Yes? Dr. Oak."

"Yes, Doc, it's Cassidy Cross. I just got my results."

"Let me just pull up your results, Cassidy. Here we go.

Yes, you are HIV negative. I'm very happy for you. Again, we do recommend more testing. I don't know if you read the letter in its entirety. It doesn't mean you're completely out of the woods, but this is a great sign, so you should be relieved."

"Yes, ma'am, I am. How do I do the other testing? When do I set it up?"

"I'd say come in to the clinic in three months. Then come three months after that. I don't recommend any sexual activity. Only abstinence keeps you completely safe from possibly spreading anything to someone else. Do you understand?" the doctor said.

"Yes, ma'am, I understand," I said and I hesitated. "My friends—you know, the three of us came in there together—I don't want to call somebody and have their results not be like mine."

"I do understand, but I cannot give out any information on another patient. Friendships are very important; you need them. You hear what I'm saying?"

"Yes, doc, I think I do."

"Okay, well, take care," she said.

As I hung up the phone, my hands started to shake. The doctor couldn't give me personal confidential information, but she had told me enough. Sister to sister, I had gotten it. One, if not both, of my girls hadn't been given the same great news I had. Now I just had to figure out what I was going to do about it. How would I want someone to deal with me if my test had come back positive? Would I want to be left alone or not?

Realizing I would want comfort, I quickly got into my car and went over to Cheryl's house. I'd be able to tell what was up without even asking her. Sure enough, when I saw her, she was open arms, hugging me, screaming until she realized she didn't know what my results said.

And then she asked, "You cool, too? Everything all right?"

"Yes!" I let out with the joy of a bride walking down the aisle.

"What about your friend—have you talked to her? You know, the girl on the dance team?" Cheryl asked.

"I'm going to go see her now," I said, realizing Ginger may need me badly.

Still happy from her news, Cheryl said, "You want me to come? I know we've all got something to celebrate. I just know it."

"No, I don't even know if she's home or whatever. You enjoy the moment," I said, trying not to give away my concern for Ginger.

"Okay, call me later. I'm so happy. I thought I was going to lose my life, Cassidy. I know I have to take some more tests, but this is good, this is great. Call me later," she said as we hugged.

Now I knew Ginger's results. What could I say to encourage her? I went over to Ginger's house and heard crying before she even came to the door.

"It's me—let me in, please. It's Cassidy." She opened the door and waited for me to give her my fate.

"Please tell me you're okay. I don't want both of us to have to go through this. I was just with him too much in the summer, I guess."

"Well, it takes only one time. Don't beat yourself up about it."

"Are you okay?" she asked, waiting for my test results to be shared.

"For now I'm negative. I do have to have other testing," I said, not trying to be too excited.

"Oh, my God, I've been praying you're okay," Ginger said unselfishly as she gave me an embrace of joy. "I don't know how I'm going to get through this. How am I going to tell my parents? What kind of future will I have?"

Smiling, I said, "You're going to be okay. They have treatment plans. What's awesome is that you know."

Trying to stay sane, Ginger said, "Yeah, I talked to Dr. Oak, and she said there's so much we'll be able to do."

"Isn't that good news?" I said as she wiped her tears.

"Yeah, I'm looking on the bright side. Thanks for coming by. You're okay, and you came by to check on me. You're a good person, Cassidy."

"I'm glad you're okay. We're both going to be okay," I said, hugging her tight.

I meant it. We were both going to be all right. I knew God had us both.

Isha and Sam were overjoyed with the fact that Cheryl and I had received great news from our tests. They took us to get ice cream. They took us to the nail shop. They took us to the movies. They just were loving on us and letting us know how happy they were for us.

I didn't take it for granted that I had friends who cared so much. And though I had personal joy, I made sure I stayed connected to Ginger as well. Everyone knew she'd been tested, and everyone knew she wasn't out around the campus celebrating and giving testimony about how she had come through this time and would make sure she was never so promiscuous again. When everyone would ask me what was up with her and what her results were, I just avoided the question, and that in and of itself gave them their answer. Ginger and I spent time on the Internet looking up information about what she was going through, and we also went to the library and found a tone of inspiring news. There was medicine she was going to be able to take on a regular basis, and just like celebrities who had come out about having HIV and had not gotten AIDS because of treatment, we felt that all hope was not lost.

I was visiting Ginger in her apartment one day when my cell rang. I looked down and was surprised to see it was Torian. What did she want with me? She and I didn't hang out, and we weren't the best of friends. I was actually shocked to get her call, and I wasn't going to answer it. But when I didn't pick it up the first time, she immediately called back again.

"Yeah?" I answered, a little huffy, letting her know she was catching me in the middle of something.

Not caring what I was doing, Torian boldly said, "We need to talk to you. We're trying to get our adviser back, and the chapter wants me to go talk to her. I'm not really down for all that. I was trying to see if you would do it."

"Are you kidding?" I let out in frustration.

She was the one who had been so vocal about getting the chapter to oust our adviser in the first place. Now she didn't think she needed to apologize? Why did she think I'd do her dirty work for her?

"Maybe that didn't come out right. I need your help, Cassidy," Torian said, understanding that she was ticking me off.

Sighing and tired of the bull, I said, "She's not going to listen to me. I tried to get her to help us before, and basically she said thanks, but no thanks. That bridge is burned for good."

"Maybe you didn't try hard enough. I know she likes you."

"That's just it, Torian, she liked all of us. We should not have let her go in the first place. Our chapter is gone, because she's not coming back," I said.

"Listen, I didn't call you to bash me. She forced my hand; she got in our business. Advisers aren't supposed to run our chapter. Really, they're supposed to advise, not demand. She crossed the line, and we—most of us—told her to leave."

"Well, then, we—most of y'all—need to tell her to come back. Maybe she'll hear you out, even though I'm sure she's heard from the state director and the Regional Coordinator to know that if y'all don't get her back, we don't have a chapter. With her knowing that, holding that card, you'll have to hold your breath. And when you hold your breath I suggest you not be under water, because when you let go, Alpha chapter will be sunk."

"Whatever. I don't even know what you're talking about."

"Don't get amnesia. You know exactly what I'm talking about. I'm not going to help you. Bye," I said, hanging up.

"I was so bummed out that I didn't pledge," Ginger

said to me, trying to help me calm down. "Now I'm going through this, and I wish I had sisters to be there for me like you're there to help me through this."

"Sisterhood is good, but sometimes, just like you have family that's crazy, you get some sisters who think you're supposed to do anything for them, and it's just not like that. You can't bail people out all the time. How are they going to learn a lesson?"

"I guess that's just it. When you truly care for people, you want to go through the hard lessons for them—I mean, I feel like I'm going through this HIV thing so you don't have to," Ginger said.

"Well, I still have more tests."

"Yeah, but there's a big chance you're fine, and that gives me hope to keep going on. I'm carrying some of the weight of it all from both of our bad choices. Shouldn't you carry some of the weight for your sisters who don't always do the right thing? We all make mistakes, but how long should we have to pay for them, you know?"

"Yeah, but you and I realized our bad choices. We were with a jerk. This girl doesn't even realize she was wrong."

"So maybe you should talk to her about that and not just turn your back and hang up on her. I don't know, forget it," Ginger said, really making me think.

Immediately, I thanked Ginger and told her to call me anytime. Soon as I got in my car, I called Torian. She met me at my house, and we had a severe heart-to-heart.

"I know I was wrong," Torian admitted. "I was just around a whole bunch of our sorors when we last talked.

I know it's stupid, but I didn't want people hearing me feel weak. However, it's killing me to know that I'm basically the reason our chapter might not be in existence anymore. People followed me, and I led them into a hot mess. I just need you to go with me to talk to her. I'll apologize. I was wrong."

I set up a meeting the next day with our ex-adviser. She heard both of us out, and Torian was surprisingly extremely forthcoming about the err of her ways. Reluctantly, our adviser agreed to come back. I learned that Ginger was right. Everyone deserves a second chance, particularly when they felt really bad for their mistake. Everything was working out for us Betas. We had unity again, and now we had an adviser. We at least had a fighting chance to stay on campus. But what would happen with Cheryl?

Another week passed, and things were coming together. I had gotten a good bill of health at least for the next couple months, I was ready for my exams, and I had great grades, so I knew my scholarship would stay intact.

My mom and I had been in contact, and she had confessed so much about her past that had been painful for her. Hearing things I didn't know was bringing us closer. She felt so bad about everything I had gone through with my uncle Bill. Like me, she and my aunt Sally were in counseling.

Also I had decided to be a drum major again. Though I enjoyed the dance team, conducting with the whole band was my skill. Working with different sections of the band and helping them get better was my strength—and the band director agreed. Plus, I knew it was Ginger's time to lead the dance team. Hopefully, this would inspire us to stay upbeat and come back to school.

But even with all that going right, I still missed Konner Black. I'd wake up in the morning, and when I'd see my toothbrush, I'd think of his perfect smile. When I went to bed at night, I'd look at my Bible and have a vision of him preaching in a pulpit, looking so good. When I was in school and going through my assignments, I would think about him studying God's word, looking adorable as he gave God first place in his life. In so many ways, I missed him. I'd left so many messages, but it'd been a few weeks since my last one.

So I went to the youth service, and after it was over and he was at his car, I walked up to him and said, "I know I pushed you away, and ever since that day you walked out of my life, I've regretted being such a fool. You haven't called me back, so I know that means you could care less about being with me anymore, and I'd be lying on church grounds if I said all I want is for us to be friends. I want more than that. Konner, I miss you."

"You don't miss me," he said, finally confirming what I knew—that it wasn't going to be easy to get him back in my life. "We didn't even really hang out that much, so it can't be that much to miss. I mean, what relationship did we really have? You shot us down before we got started."

He started fidgeting with his car door. I walked over to him and touched his hand. When he turned and looked at me, I knew I had to tell him all I felt inside.

So I touched his face and said, "It's like how I felt accepting Christ into my heart. It didn't take a lot of time. It was just an instant feeling that changed me. And being with you is something that I want—no, that I need in my life. And if I'm wrong, if there isn't a genuine true concern for me on your part, I'll leave you alone. But I know you care. You've showed it and revealed it too much for it not to be true. Though I've wounded you by not accepting your heart, I'm asking for grace. I'm asking for you to give me a chance to love you back."

He looked over at me and said nothing. His eyes were squinted, so I knew he was aggravated with me. I took that as a sign that maybe I had pushed him to a point where he could not forgive me, ever, so I turned and slowly walked away.

He grabbed my hand and then put his hands around my waist and said, "If God can see us from up above, I'd be lying to tell you that I don't care about you, that I don't think about you, that I don't want us to be together."

"I'm not perfect, Konner," I said, tears welling up in my eyes.

Gently stroking my face, he said, "I'm not perfect either."

"I did have the test. For now, I'm okay, but I don't know if I'm going to be okay, really. I got to go back and get tested again in a few months," I said, letting him fully understand all that came with dealing with me.

"And as I told you before, if you have something, we'll go through it together. I want to be in a relationship with you. I'm not your sorority sister or your mom, so in no way are we family, but in my heart we've got a bond," he said as he touched his chest. "I prayed you'd come back to me."

Thinking I may end up hurting him, I said, "You could have so many other women—so many who are good, kind, and pure."

"Like I said, your coming here tonight is the answer to my prayer. I don't know how things will work out—I mean, we're just starting this thing again. But this is something I want. For a second chance, I'm grateful."

18

PURE

"I can't believe we're actually going through with this. I mean, whose idea was it to have a Bible study?" Torian said as our sorors filed into our chapter room.

Yeah, we were having a Bible study, and I had called it. Malloy had charged me and my line sisters with coming up with new programs, things that would have a purpose and make a difference. We had been through so much turmoil ever since we had crossed. We really hadn't focused on anything meaningful. But I no longer wanted to be just a member of Beta Gamma Pi. I wanted to make a difference, add to its value of work, and contribute. I wanted to work, and our biggest problem right now was that we were still divided; we wanted different things. I knew the only way we could agree was to follow in God's grace.

I just kept overhearing Torian in the corner talking

smack. She was being so condescending it was working my last nerve. She needed to quit being negative.

I went over to her and said, "Can I see you out in the hall for a second?"

"This is supposed to start at two; it is one fifty-one. We don't have time to go out into the hall. You called this Bible study together, so you need to hurry and get started," Torian responded as she flung her head away from me.

"Can I see you out in the hall for a second?" I repeated with my nostrils flared. She followed me out of the room.

"What's going on? What do you want now?" she asked.

"I'm just going to cut to the chase," I said.

"All right, I'm listening."

"Why are you speaking your mind and being so pessimistic?"

"I can say what I wanna say!" she said sharply to me.

I took a deep breath because I realized I had the wrong approach. In order for her to hear what I truly had to say, I couldn't be so offensive or stoop to her level. So, not being phony or fake, I found the words to get her to listen. Touching her shoulder, I said, "Torian, you are a leader."

"I know that. What else do you have to say?" she said in a softer tone.

"Whatever you're thinking or feeling, you put it out there for the sorors, and they take it in. They take it to heart. They wanna take the action you want them to take."

"Yeah, you're right," she said, cocky and confident.

"And all I'm asking is for you to give this whole Bible-study thing a try. Our sorority was founded on Christian beliefs and values. Right now we're going through a lot of drama, and we need God. We all need to do better. You asked for my help with the adviser and I was there. Now I'm asking for your help to not shoot this down before we even give it a try."

"People don't listen to me like that," she said, trying to downplay what I was asking her to do.

"Yes, they do. And I just think if we listen to God's Word, it will help us. Miracles will happen, and He will show us the way. I'm not trying to sound all spiritual and everything," I said to her because she was looking at me like *What is wrong with you?* "But I believe that from the bottom of my heart."

"All right, I appreciate you coming to me. You're honest. I can back off and not put roadblocks on your route to God's grace. Come on," Torian said as she tugged me back in the room.

The vibe in the room had changed—Torian's opinion was contagious. People were downplaying the idea of Bible study to each other. Some of the folks who were down for it—like Malloy, Alyx, and Sam—came running up to me saying maybe this wasn't a good idea.

Torian surprised me by saying, "All right, everybody, hush up! I was wrong at first for going against this Bible-study thing, but we need this. Cassidy, go ahead and lead us, girl."

I couldn't argue with her at all. Everyone shut up and pulled out her Bible or shared someone else's. Hoping I'd make a difference, I began.

"I chose a scripture from Proverbs chapter twenty-three, verse seven. We are such strong-willed women.

The Word says, *As a man thinketh, so is He*. If we want our chapter to be saved, we must figure out a way to still stay loyal to Cheryl. We should think about how to do the right things and what Jesus would do. As Philippians chapter four, verse eight says, *Whatever is just, whatever is pure, and whatever is lovely—think on these things*. If we get rid of the negative thoughts about each other, about our circumstances, about what we can't do, and focus on the good, we will see better results."

They stood and gave me a round of applause. Isha came over and closed us out with a prayer. God was at work when we stopped and gave Him reverence.

Unfortunately, as soon as the prayer was over, we did have to deal with the reality of what we were going to tell the school. Our adviser was in the room. We asked her for advice on how we should go about doing so, and she didn't say anything. She wanted us to try to work it out. She had learned that dictating, telling us what we should and should not do, versus allowing us to get to the best decision on our own, was not the best action when it came to leading a group of college-educated women.

Torian stood and said, "I love each of you guys, but if I did something wrong, my love is so real that I wouldn't let you take the fall for it."

She got a lot of "Amens" and "I know that's right" from the crowd.

Then Loni stood and said, "I hear what you're saying, girl, but if we don't protect each other, do we really have a sorority? We're supposed to be our sisters' keeper, and if we sell Cheryl down the river, we're out for ourselves and not Alpha chapter. I just think there's gotta be another way. If Cheryl's not willing to come forward, we have to protect her. Isn't that what honor is all about?"

Some sorors agreed with her viewpoint as well. What were we going to do? Like a math division problem with a horrendous remainder, we weren't dividing evenly.

Then all of a sudden Cheryl appeared from the back of the room. "But I *am* willing to come forward, and like Torian said, I have a responsibility not to just feel love for you guys but to love you back and do what's right. You shouldn't have to be separated, trying to figure out this whole situation with me. I plan to leave this meeting and go with you guys to meet with President Webb."

"You can't do that." Sam rushed over to her. "You'll get expelled. You might go to jail. You were depressed. It wasn't your fault what you did to Meagan. We got your back."

Isha stood and said, "We're willing to have your back, but it's you on the line. Alpha chapter is bigger than any of us, but we care for you. What do you really want to do?"

Cheryl said, "I want to report what I did now. I want to save our chapter."

I was sitting next to our Dr. Garnes. She leaned over and mumbled to me, "Wow! Look at how God can work things out."

Sam started crying. "Why are you gonna do this?"

Cheryl put her arm around Sam. "I can deal with going to jail and not being at Western Smith—those things are bad. But dying could be worse, and God gave me a gift. At least, for right now, I'm okay. So I wanna honor Him by giving Him some of the things that mattered to me. If I can't be a part of this chapter, that's the price I'm gonna have to pay, but at least I can be excited knowing that I didn't hurt the chapter for good. Who wouldn't want to be a part of a group of women who will stand up for you? Even those of you who wanna tell hadn't to this point, and I take your loyalty seriously. It matters to me, and it has helped get me through my own personal tough time. But now that that's passed, now that you've done your part and God has given me a gift, we need to get out of here and go see the President. I just have one request."

"Name it," Malloy said, excitedly speaking for us all.

"When you get the chapter out of the danger zone, when the sorority pardons you guys and gives you a clean bill of health to keep operating, when the new school year starts in a few months, remember to treat Beta Gamma Pi right. Remember that everything you do reflects on our chapter. Do a project where you tell teens about the consequences of premarital sex. Lastly, remember to please God because if you strive to hit His mark, you'll be in the clear."

We all rushed up and hugged her and then went to handle our business with the President. After a little Bible study, God had showed us He could fix it.

A couple weeks had passed. We were finished with exams. We'd gotten a clearance from the school and the sorority, so Alpha chapter was fine. We'd still be on probation for another year because we had violated the probation this year, but at least we were moving forward and we weren't closed down. Like Cheryl had reminded us, we all vowed to take good care of our chapter with this next chance we had been given.

Also, Meagan had dropped the charges against Cheryl, so Cheryl didn't have to go to jail. We found out Meagan was also clear of HIV and had been feeling Cheryl's same state of mind the night of the fight. I guess she understood what the whole ordeal was about and was thankful that she, too, had a clean bill of health.

As far as Cheryl and school, she was going to be suspended for a semester. She also would be out of the sorority and have to pay a fine of one thousand dollars for misrepresenting the sisterhood of Beta Gamma Pi. Cheryl was fine with all those things. Like me, she was just happy that God had spared her life, and she was going to do everything she could not to let him down again.

Konner and I were doing great as well. We were taking things slow, not getting too close physically, and being real with our time together. He talked about his hopes, fears, and dreams, and I did the same. We talked about wanting to get a degree, and we worked it out so he could go to a junior college in the fall.

Sam, Isha, and I were excited to be at the National Convention. Malloy's mom had one more year of being President. The church service that had been held on the Saturday evening of the convention had been moving. The National Chaplain, Bishop Volante Taylor, had notoriety. She'd won the Nobel Peace Prize six years before for her work in Africa. She was the author of several books and gave lectures across the country. She was also the bishop for five churches in the DC area and was rumored to be going into politics. Women were dominating the nation one speech at a time.

"Come on, Cassidy. We have to go get a good seat," Isha said.

Then Sam came running up to us. "Where are we gonna sit? It is cold as ice in here. I hope this ceremony doesn't take long, because I have to get back to the room and pack."

I just looked over at her. "After all we've been through this year, the Lord has moved and shown Himself to be faithful. We're able to be at this convention because He didn't allow us to be kicked off campus and out of the sorority. If we had to sit here all day with coats on and praise His name, that wouldn't be enough."

"You're right, you're right," Sam said.

Bishop Taylor took to the mic and said, "I won't be up here long. We've had a great convention, good workshops, good speeches, and a good time all around. I just want to spread a word of hope. You all have it going on. We are sisters of Beta Gamma Pi, the most powerful sorority in the world. We don't just talk about things happening, we envision them happening, work to make them happen, and come out successful in the end. I want to talk to you about Daniel in the Lions' Den this evening. You see, Daniel was a young man who was facing adversity, but he didn't look at adversity as a sign of hopelessness. He looked at adversity as his friend. And that's the message of this evening. Adversity is your friend. We got it going on as sisters of Beta Gamma Pi because we want the challenge to be brought on. You might say, 'Well,

Bishop Taylor, how is adversity our friend?' Well, I have three points for you."

Sam nudged me in the arm and said, "Yeah, how is adversity your friend? I can't stand adversity. I pray next year that Alpha chapter will be drama free. Let's just serve others. No parties, just service," she joked, having been selected as our new President. "First Vice, are you down with the service?"

I nodded. As far as the adversity thing went, I was saying the same thing in my head—*I hate adversity*. But as I looked back over my year at Western Smith, I saw that I had started out not caring about myself and I had gone through a journey to find out why I was that way—and had become better because of it. God had brought me through with flying colors. If I was better only because I'd gone through the storm, I didn't wanna have to go through another to make me stronger.

Soror Taylor continued. "One: Adversity makes you face the truth. You need to look at yourself, look around you, and shave off the things that aren't working. Sorors, cut the baggage. Better yourself. Straighten up! The time is now; you can't do big things if you're in denial. Number two: Adversity makes you figure it out. When you're up against the rope—you have no way out, no hope, no solution—adversity draws you to your knees, and you come to God. And then He can reign and rule in your life, and He can give you a plan. Trust Him, sorors. Trust Him. And, finally: Adversity helps you finish standing. We celebrate triumphs because someone went through something, and they came out strong. Betas do big things because we aren't afraid to back down from the hard stuff. Adversity is your friend, sorors. Go back to your campus and continue to make a difference. Be better. Be stronger. Face the truth, figure it out, and finish standing."

We all rose to our feet and shouted excitedly. We were inspired, we were encouraged, and we were ready to move the sorority forward. Yeah, we were all the bomb, but we had to remember to keep God first like Bishop Taylor had said.

This year I had learned that when people thought they had it going on, they got the big head. But the only thing that will keep you humble is lifting Him up. Bring your sorrows to Him, bring your troubles to Him, bring your desires to Him, bring your triumphs to Him, bring your fears to Him, bring it all to Him because He'll help you through it. And at the end of the day, when there is no one else you can turn to, God has your heart, and even through your sin, His grace can make you pure.

Beta Gamma Pi, Book 4:

Got It Going On

Stephanie Perry Moore

ABOUT THIS GUIDE

The following questions are intended to
enhance your group's reading of
Beta Gamma Pi: GOT IT GOING ON
by Stephanie Perry Moore

DISCUSSION QUESTIONS

1. Cassidy Cross wants to be noticed at the Beta Gamma Pi opening bash, and she is, but only because she was acting wildly. Do you think she was sending out the wrong message? Why do you feel some people try hard to fit in to make people think they have it going on?

2. Cassidy's date with Al Dutch goes too far. If you're not ready to take the next step in your relationship, how would you tell your partner?

3. Cassidy is depressed for a while after her incident with Al Dutch, so she seeks help from a psychiatrist. Do you think this was a good idea? Why or why not?

4. At the rush, Cassidy knows her stuff. Do you think the Betas were impressed with her knowledge of their history, and what do you think the other interested girls were thinking? When you are trying to be a part of a group, what are ways you can be prepared?

5. The girls' line is divided when some want to be hazed and others don't. Do you feel it was right or wrong for Cassidy to stand her ground? What are better ways to settle differences?

6. Cassidy starts having nightmares and flashbacks of images she can't completely explain. Do you think it was right that she kept this from her roommate and everyone else? When you feel you're in too deep, to whom do you turn for help?

7. Cassidy misses lots of events. Do you feel it was great that her sorority sisters found her and got her professional help? Do you think dealing with your past is healthy for your future?

8. Al Dutch reveals he is HIV positive. Though Cassidy is scared, she ultimately gets tested for HIV. How can being properly informed help you?

9. Cassidy tells Konner of her situation. Do you believe it is honorable for him to still want to be involved with her even though they don't know her fate? What types of qualities do you want the person you're in a relationship with to have?

10. Cassidy and her sorority sisters go through much but come out tighter in the end. Does it seem that once they turned things over to God, things worked out for them? Do you feel that having the Lord in the midst of all you do can make the biggest impact?

Stay tuned for the next book in the series,
GET WHAT YOU GIVE,
available May 2010, wherever books are sold.
Until then, satisfy your Beta Gamma Pi craving with
the following excerpt from the next installment.

ENJOY!

BABBLE

"Would you risk your own life to possibly try to save someone else's? People talk about best friends, including you, Hailey Grant, but would you really lay it all on the line to make sure your best friend was spared from pain?" my roommate, Teddi Spencer, rambled on as I tried to study. "I mean, 'cause you're not acting like it."

What was she talking about? We were tighter than tight, and she knew I had her back. But every now and then when I wasn't doing something she thought I should, she'd try to lay a guilt trip on me. So I kept on studying and ignored her tail, hoping she'd get the picture and shut up.

Actually, most of the folks who had known us all last year wondered why we were even friends. We were pretty different. I was about facts, and she was about fiction.

There was nothing wrong with dreaming, but you had to get your head out of the clouds if you wanted to actually get things done. I swear, her address was La-La Land. She irked my nerves all the time, but I knew I could never intentionally walk out of her life. Teddi had lost more in her high school years than my heart could bear. If being my friend made her happy and gave her joy, I'd do anything to protect that.

"I'm just saying. I gotta win the election, Hailey. And you're not helping. That guy Colvin—Calvin—Compton—whatever his name is—thinks just because he's the state senator's son, everybody's on his jock. Well, I'm . . ." I finally tuned Teddi out when she began talking about her disgust for her rival SGA opponent in the upcoming election.

I looked at my short, frail, light-skinned friend. She had been through so much over the past two years I've known her. We were now sophomores at Western Smith College. When she'd lost her parents in a tragic car accident her senior year, she'd moved in with her grandmother and begun attending my high school.

She hadn't known anybody, and she'd seemed like she was in deep pain. I had taken it upon myself to help and befriend her. I didn't know where that had come from—you know, the knack to want to help someone out. I guess somewhere deep inside me there is a place that feels I should give back because I've been taken care of all my life. I have two great parents. My uncle is the president of the college I attend, for goodness' sake. My older sister went to college at Western Smith, and everyone remembered what a gem she'd been. Honestly, I'm no princess, but I haven't had any tragedies in my life either. Because I can clearly identify that I am who I am because of the people in my life, I guess I feel the need to help those who have no one.

Teddi sat on my bed next to me in our dorm room and turned my face toward her. "You're not even listening to me, Hailey. I mean, I need to win this election. It's time for a female to take charge, and I'm the right person for the position, especially after all the drama we faced with the last President. They need to feel confident in the new President, and, personally, I don't think anyone comes close to me."

"What are you saying, Teddi? We need a female President?" I asked. I mean, it would be cool to have a female President, but that shouldn't be the only reason she should run.

I guess Teddi didn't like my response, 'cause she got a little loud with me and said, "You got a problem with that? You don't think I'm strong enough, do you? You don't think I can lead? I mean, why would any of us females around here trust someone who leads by what's between his legs, like our old President Al Dutch?"

"No, no. I'm just saying that just because one male was stupid doesn't mean the others have to be the same."

Teddi paced back and forth, freaking out. "Well, I'm just saying we need a change, and you're completely not behind me. My campaign manager isn't on my side."

"Why are you overexaggerating the issue?"

"Because we need to come up with a strategy. I've seen

posters all over campus for this guy, and my posters aren't even up yet. Isn't that your job?" my ungrateful roommate and best buddy uttered.

Quickly, I reminded her she was the reason we hadn't gotten a lot accomplished with her campaign. "Listen, chick. I love you, but you're full of it. Every idea I've had, you've shot down. It's your fault you don't have a platform. I drill you on the basic questions, like 'Why do you want to be the SGA President,' and you stutter and say, 'Because we don't need a male.' That's bull. I can't put out material on your campaign when you have no legit ideas. What do you expect?"

Teddi sank to her bed and played the victim role. "Then say I'm just a loser. Quit my campaign. Don't help me."

"Oh, girl, don't be melodramatic. I know you have substance. Find it and let's get a plan. I've seen the posters of the guy running. People in the dorm have been hovering around them. But we can get yours out," I said, trying to let her know I wasn't planning to bail, but if she wanted to win, we needed to get cracking.

Can't get enough of sorority life?
Turn the page for more of Stephanie Perry Moore's
Beta Gamma Pi series,
available now wherever books are sold.

From *Work What You Got*

BRIGHT

"So you think it's okay if somebody whacks you up-side the head, calls you all kinds of names, beats your behind, and who knows whatever else, Hayden Grant? I've even heard of cases where sororities make pledges perform some kind of sexual act," my mom Shirley voiced in anger, as my caramel face turned pale.

"Mom! I can't believe you would go there with me."

"What, Hayden? Don't be shocked. I know how bad you want to be a Beta and I know you might lose your mind to get what you want. Plus, you're about to be a sophomore in college, at a predominately African-American school. I know there are several nice-looking young men around grabbing your attention. Something made your grades slip last semester. I think you're still pure, but we need to talk about sex."

"I can't talk about this with my mom. I just can't," I said, shyly turning my head and twirling my mid-length do.

"Better she talk about it with you," my sister, younger by four years, popped into my room and said.

"Hailey, have you been standing there the whole time? Quit being nosy," my mom scolded and shooed her away.

"We were talking about being a Beta, Mom. We weren't talking about me and sex," I quickly reminded her.

"Well, I'm not done. I think any young lady that makes smart choices will do that across the board. If you make wise decisions, particularly when the alternative is giving it up to some boy who the next day probably won't know you exist. You could wind up pregnant or with some disease. Isn't it better to stay away from all that? Someone who's strong enough to resist temptation and stands for what God says is right, will not want to be a part of some group that thinks the only way you can get in is to participate in some form of illegal activity that the organization doesn't even tolerate," she said, getting louder and louder with each sentence.

"Okay Mom, I get it! You don't have to go on and on and on about it," I said to her, extremely frustrated.

I didn't want to go there with her, but it seemed to me like she needed to get her groove on. My dad Harry was away at war. He's an officer in the Navy and his girl had too much idle time on her hands. So much so that she was all up in my business.

My mom knew I wanted to be a member of Beta Gamma Pi ever since she pledged the organization's alumnae chapter when I was in the fifth grade. After she became a member, I remember many nights during my childhood when she was away with the service-oriented organization, working in the community by taking food to the poor, being there for the elderly, and helping the uneducated gain knowledge. Even though part of me resented not having all of her time, it just fueled me, excited me, and made me want to strive to become a member one day. My mom had wanted to pledge as an undergraduate when she was in college, but due to females tripping, she didn't. I had a deep longing to obtain that goal for her.

My mom came over and got right in my face. "Let me just tell you this really quickly. I desperately want you to be a Beta. But if you participate in any of that foolishness and anything happens, I don't want you calling me. I don't want you thinking that I can help save the line. None of that. Do you understand? I'm telling you now, I don't support hazing and in the end it only divides. Be a leader on that campus, Hayden Grant."

She went on to explain, for the fiftieth time, the legitimate steps to becoming a Beta. First, there was rush, where an informational session is held and the members of the organization explain all about what they stand for and what they do. They also distribute application packets to the prospective candidates, which need to be turned in by a certain date. After the packets are returned and reviewed by the members of the organization, then comes the interview. But not everyone will get one. After the interview, if you receive enough votes from the sisters of Beta Gamma Pi, then you become a part of the pledge line. After handing in the money for the pledge fee, a Pi induction ceremony is held. There are five gem ceremonies and an Eagle weekend hosted by the alumnae chapter, which pledges must attend. Next there is an intense week of studying the history of the sorority and a major exam is given before the candidates are ready to cross over and become sisters of Beta Gamma Pi.

"You participate in any other activity and it's hazing. Got it?"

I nodded. Of course I heard her, but I couldn't say what I would and wouldn't do once pressure from the Betas was applied. I didn't want to be ostracized and considered paper because I wouldn't participate in a few little uncomfortable things. I mean how bad could hazing really be, right?

There are certain rules that go along with the way many people think is the best way to pledge. First, pledging on the collegiate level carries more weight than pledging in an alumnae chapter. I thought this was crazy. However, the rationale is that collegiate chapters really make members do things *way* over and above what the standard rules call for. Also, many believe that if you don't go through the collegiate process then you are not a real pledge, only a *paper* one. And let's face it, if you have the chance, who wants to be called paper? Definitely not me.

Then there is the legacy rule. In some sororities if your mother is a member and you have the qualifications, then there is no vote necessary. You automatically become a member. But, with Beta Gamma Pi, that isn't the case. Since my mom didn't pledge on the collegiate level, their preferred methods, I knew I was going to have to pay for what she didn't go through. I was ready for it, because I knew if I made line I could legitimize my mom's place in the sorority.

"I'm gonna make you proud, Mom. You don't have to worry," I said, stroking her verbally and psychologically.

"Honey, all you need to do is concentrate on your grades and be the best Hayden you know how to be. If the Betas don't want you, it's their loss. You can always pledge the way I did," she said in a sweet tone, so I'd keep my hope. But I wasn't having it.

My mom wasn't all excited about the way she pledged. She knew the stigma attached to alumnae pledge methods. Though I knew deep in my heart that being put through an intense pledge process didn't make one a better member, if I had the opportunity to get all my props, I had to do it. Why would she think I wouldn't want all the respect?

My mother continued, "Now see, I can tell by your face you think pledging on the alumnae level is not kosher."

"Well, it was your dream to pledge undergrad," I quickly reminded her.

"Yeah, but just because that didn't work out doesn't mean that I would go back and trade my experience for anything. I was so connected with the ladies on my line. And quite honestly it was absolutely the best timing. God knew what He was doing. And Hayden, for you to have the outcome that He wants for your life, you have to ignore what others say and just focus on what is right. You know how to be a strong person, but a strong leader knows that God's way is golden. So seek Him and figure out what He wants for you. Plus, I truly now believe pledging on an alumnae level is the best way to join the organization," she said with her worried eyes locked on mine.

I smiled, feeling she believed those last words. I hugged

her to let her know though I wanted a different experience, I was going to be okay. Then I was off to college. Western Smith College, here I come.

We hugged, and then I was off. It was time to get my sophomore year started.

From *The Way We Roll*

BECOMING

If I see one more Beta Gamma Pi girl looking down at me because I'm not sporting any of them pitiful letters, I might just kick her tail. Yes, I'm here at their convention, but I am not Greek. I'm not here like other wannabes; I'm here because I have to be.

My mom, Dr. Monica Jenkins Murray, is their National President, and that makes me sick. I can't believe my time with my mom has taken a backseat to the sorority. For real, when it came to my mom doing sorority business versus my mom being a mom, I came last every time. Yeah, she said all the sorority stuff was for the good of the community and one day I'd understand her sacrifice, but when she didn't make any of my piano recitals or parent-teacher conferences, I started to detest the group she loved.

After my parents divorced and my older brother moved out with my dad, it was just my mom and me. Though we lived in the same house, we were worlds apart. Basically I felt Beta Gamma Pi took everything away from me. I was at the National Convention only because some of the ladies on the executive board were more of a mom to me than my own mother. The First Vice President, Deborah Day, who lived in California, begged me to come support their endeavors. Because she was always there when I needed someone to talk to, I came. Plus, the VIP rooms in the hotel were stocked with alcohol. With no one around to supervise, I was feeling nice.

"You're all smiles. I guess you just finished kissing the National President's butt, huh?" I said to a girl coming out of my mom's presidential suite.

"I'm sorry, do I know you?" the girl said, squinting, trying to figure out who I was.

"You're so full of it," I said, calling her out as I stumbled, trying to get my key to work on the door. "You know who I am. You're just trying to get on my good side to raise your stock with her."

The girl persisted. "I'm sorry, I'm not trying to offend you, but you really do look familiar. Do you need some help with that?"

I snatched my hand away. "I don't need your help."

"What's going on out here?" The door flung open, and my mom came out in the hallway.

"I was, uh, trying to get in the room." I fell back a little.

"Girl, you are so embarrassing me. Get your drunk behind in here now," my mom said sternly. Then she sweetly spoke to the other girl. "Hayden, come in, please."

"Wasn't she just leaving?" I said. I was so confused. My mom went over to this Hayden girl and just started explaining my behavior, like she needed to apologize to some college girl about how I was acting. Why couldn't my mom apologize to me that I had to put up with a brownnoser?

"Come here, Malloy, I want to introduce you guys," my mom said. I reluctantly walked over to them. "Hayden Grant, this is my daughter Malloy Murray. Malloy, Hayden is the Chapter President of Beta Gamma Pi on your campus."

"See, I thought I knew you." The girl smiled, and she reached to shake my hand. "I'm going to be a junior. I knew I'd seen you around school, but I didn't know this was your mom."

"Yeah, sure you didn't know this was my mom," I said sarcastically while keeping my arms glued to my sides.

My mom huffed, "Lord, you don't have to be rude."

"Then don't force me to talk to someone I don't want to talk to, and don't apologize for how I'm feeling. I have a right to be angry, okay, Mom? I don't want to embarrass you anymore, so please get this girl out of my face. I don't care what school she goes to. Unlike both of you, I don't think Beta Gamma Pi is God's gift to the world."

"Hayden, I'm so sorry about this again. Let's just keep this between us. My daughter doesn't usually drink. She'll be much more herself when you guys get back to school. Let's just say I do look forward to working more closely with your chapter, particularly when Malloy makes line."

"Yes, ma'am," Hayden said, really getting on my nerves. She could not get out of the suite fast enough for me. Of course, after she left, my mom looked at me like she was disappointed. Shucks, I was the one rightfully upset. The alcohol just allowed me to finally let out how I felt.

"Mom, don't go making no promises to that girl about me being on line. I'm in school to get an education, not to pledge. Plus, their last line was crazy. They haze up there. You want me to have something to do with that? You're the National President. You're supposed to be against any form of hazing. I'm telling you it was all around school that they put a girl from the last line in the hospital."

She looked at me and rolled her eyes. I believed what I was saying. Some of those girls would do anything to wear Greek letters. Not me.

Changing her tone, she said, "Sweetheart, if you're a part of it, they won't do anything like that. I don't have to worry about anybody doing anything you don't want, as tough as you are. Just promise me you'll take this into consideration. This is one of my hopes for you, Malloy. Being a part of this sisterhood can be so fulfilling. You don't even have a best friend, for crying out loud."

"Yeah, for crying out loud, one of your biggest dreams for me is to be in a sorority. Not to fall in love with a man and stay married forever—like you couldn't. Not to graduate from college with honors and get a great job or doctorate—like you did. Instead, you're praying your child gets into a sorority. I might have had a couple drinks, but it's clear to me that's the thing you want most for me." I plopped down on the couch, picked up the remote, clicked on the television, and put the volume on high. "Don't hold your breath on me becoming a Beta. Sweet dreams, Mommy."

She went into her part of the suite and slammed the door. I knew I had disappointed her. However, as much as she had disappointed me in my life, we weren't anywhere close to being even.

From *Act Like You Know*

BARRIER

"Alyx Cruz in the house. I'm a Beta Gamma Pi girl—get out the way! Alyx Cruz in the house. I'm a Beta Gamma Pi girl—I work it all day!" I chanted as I swayed my Latina hips from left to right at the National Convention's collegiate party for my beloved sorority, Beta Gamma Pi.

I wasn't trying to be funny or anything, but as a Mexican in a black sorority, it was not easy. I had it going on. The looks I got from men told me they wanted to get with me, and the looks I got from girls told me they wanted to be me, or they hated me because they weren't. It wasn't my fault that I didn't have kinky hair and that mine flowed more like a white girl's (though, truth be told, some days I wished mine was kinky—maybe then I'd fit in with everyone). Though they couldn't see it, I felt like a true sister from my core. But most Betas felt a

Spanish girl shouldn't be in a predominantly African American sorority. If they'd take time to get to know me they'd see I was down for the same things they were. That's why I joined Beta Gamma Pi.

However, if another one of my sorors looked at me like they wanted to snatch my letters off my chest, they were gonna be in for war—a real fight. I hated that I'd had to transfer to a new school. I'd finally gotten people to like me for me back in Texas, but because I'd partied just a little too much—okay, well, not just a little too much, a lot too much—my grades had suffered. And I'd put my scholarship in jeopardy. It was a minority scholarship, for which you had to maintain a 3.0 grade point average. I'd had to find another school that would take me with my 2.6 GPA, but I'd wished I could fix my mistakes. I hoped I wouldn't squander another great opportunity.

Now I was gonna have to start all over again winning friends at Western Smith College, my Tio Pablo's alma mater. My uncle helped my mom and me come to the United States from Mexico when I was three. He'd died when I was six, and it had been me and my mom ever since. My mom kept his framed degree in our house to inspire me to do more. So I applied to Western Smith and thankfully got enough financial aid to attend.

I couldn't get an education any other way. I had an opportunity, and I couldn't be crazy with it. I had to make sure I seized the chance. Here I was in America living the dream, and I had been about to waste all that. But now at Western Smith, I had a second chance.

But I couldn't focus on any of that, particularly when my favorite song came on. "Hey, get 'em up, get 'em up!"

I started shouting as I turned, swiveled, sashayed, and bumped into that girl Malloy I'd met an hour before.

"I am so sorry," I stuttered, taken aback at seeing Malloy with about fifteen of her buddies all staring hard at me like I'd stolen their men or something.

"Oh, no, you're fine. It's perfect anyway. I was just telling my chapter sorors here about you," Malloy said in an overly sweet tone.

All these girls were from the Alpha chapter at Western Smith, where my sorority was founded. For some reason the girls in this chapter really thought they were better than everybody else. I could tell by the way they looked at me that they wished I'd go crawl under a rock. But I was on my way to their campus, and I already had my letters, so they needed to get over themselves. I looked at them, my hand on my hip and my eyes fully awake, like, "What . . . what you gon' do?"

"*Okayyy,* let's have some hugs and some love," Malloy said as she pushed me toward them.

The hugs I got from some of the girls made me want to throw up. They were so fake with it. When I got to the last few, I didn't even move to hug them. I wasn't a pledge. They could respect me or keep stepping. A few of the girls turned their noses up at me and walked off. I didn't care, because the sorors I pledged with would always be there for me when I needed sisterhood.

Then Malloy touched my shoulder and whispered, "Wait, please let me introduce you. Please."

Something in her gesture got to me. I didn't know her from Adam, but she was genuine. I really appreciated her wanting to make the awkwardness dissolve.

"These are my line sisters Torian and Loni"—neither girl standing next to her said hello—"our Chapter President, Hayden Grant; Bea, our First Vice President, and Sharon." Those three didn't even put up our sign, which was customary when you met a new soror.

"Now y'all, for real, you're being rude," Malloy scolded as she turned her back to me and tried to get her chapter sorors straight.

She didn't have to go defending me. I could hold my own. Shoot, they didn't want me in their chapter. Well, too doggone bad. I was coming, and what were they going to do about it?

But then, as I saw them continuously staring, I realized they were seriously feeling threatened. They didn't know me or my heart. I had to make them feel comfortable and let them know I wasn't trying to mess up their game. So I said, "Hey, I know it's tough accepting an outsider into your fold, but in my soul let me say I feel like family. I mean, I am your soror. I know a lot of Betas who aren't really excited about Spanish girls, but trust me, I don't want the spotlight, and my letters didn't come easy—I was hazed. I just want us to be cool, all right?"

Bea smiled and stuck out her hand for me to dap. When the others girls smiled as well—I guess now they knew I wasn't paper—we were cool.

"To me, more importantly than how I pledged is why I pledged," I continued sincerely. "I plan to make a difference in the community and I love this organization. Just give me a chance."

All the girls finally gave me a real embrace. I didn't know where we'd go from here, but I was excited to find out.